CHAPTER I

HAPPY NEW YEAR

" I feel like I'm living in a bubble—an actual bubble." I narrow my eyes at Dr. Herman, searching for any flicker of recognition on his clinical face. But the slight crease forming between his brows tells me he's not quite following.

I wave my hands in front of me, drawing an imaginary circle in the air, hoping to drive the point home. "There's this bubble, right? I'm stuck inside it. Meanwhile, everything—my job, my apartment, my friends, even my parents' deaths—they're all on the outside, pressed up against the walls. Just staring at me, like hawks. You know?"

I squint harder, trying to gauge if he understands.

"What do you mean?" he asks, keeping that

stoic, *I'm the shrink—you're the crazy person* look plastered across his face.

I glare at him, biting back the urge to snap. It's such a textbook question. *What do I mean?* He knows. He's just dragging it out of me for the sake of the session. But I answer anyway. "Take you, for example. You're part of the bubble too."

"In what way?"

I exhale hard, shifting in my seat. "Well... you're just another perfectly placed piece in this Lego world I'm stuck in. Like, where do you live, Dr. Herman? Are you married? Where were you even born? Are you... are you even real?"

Time feels static as I wait for him to answer at least one of those questions. I really need to know if I'm crazy or sane. While I wait for his reply, I notice how chilly it is in here. It's snowing outside. Herman's the kind of individual who never turns up the heater high enough, which is one of the reasons why I hate coming here, especially during the winter. Though I've never asked him to turn up the thermostat for my comfort. Something about feeling cold settles me when things get tight, and I *do* know why.

"Well, let's talk about your parents," he says.

I'm not surprised that he chose not to answer

THE FIFTH SISTER

PARCHED
BOOK FOUR

Z.L. ARKADIE

FLAMING
HEARTS

ISBN: 978-1-942857-59-4

any of my direct questions, but mentioning my parents always captures my full attention. I raise an eyebrow. "What about them?"

"They died ten years ago, and yet you just mentioned them in the scope of your present life, including me." He crosses his legs and leans against one arm of his squishy faux leather armchair as he studies me. "You once said that you felt indifferent about your parents' death. Has that changed?"

I look at my feet. There's a clear stain on my brand-new tan snow boots. I must've dropped a speck of maple syrup on them this morning. I work at an all-night diner, which has the ambiance of a café. I don't need to work. When my parents died, I received a lot of money from the life insurance policy. I don't know exactly how much. I mostly live off my salary and tips. But here's the deal, I chose to work at the diner just to remind myself that I have contact from inside the bubble with real people. When they leave my sight, I'm alone again in Lego Land.

"Nothing's changed," I mutter, and I'm sort of ashamed of it too.

"Did you feel indifferent about them when they were alive?"

Funny, I've been coming here for four years, and he's never asked me that question.

"They were okay, I guess" is my pathetic answer.

"I didn't ask how they were as parents. I asked—"

"I know," I say with a sigh. "You asked if I felt indifferent about them."

A lot about my parents, Charles and Rachel Slater, was borderline *Twilight Zone*. I've listened to some of my customers talk about their parents. I've seen a lot of families come into the diner, occupy a table, and act normal. The kid climbs all over the chairs and tables. The mother constantly says don't do this or that until she can no longer take it, and then out of nowhere, she explodes and yells, "Sit your ass down!" The kid gets the sniffles. The mom feels guilty. The kid gets all the ice cream and whipped cream he can cram down his throat. Rachel Slater would've never exploded. I, as a kid, would've never driven her to that point. My whole life, we were the *blah* family.

"I don't know," I say. "I feel okay about them now."

"What do you mean by *okay*?"

"Well, my mom was a master of good housekeeping. She put Donna Reed to shame. And my dad was the king of traveling salesmen. He was never home. When he did show up, he'd read a paper all morning and mow the lawn in the afternoon. Sometimes he'd ask me how my day went, but I always felt like he didn't really want to know the answer. I felt like he was living by a script that said, 'Give the kid a little attention after you read the paper. Now take out the trash and mow the lawn. Kiss the wife at six p.m. Tell the girl, "Goodnight, sweet dreams, and I'll call you in a few days."' All scripted."

"And did he? Call you in a few days?"

"Of course. Don't *you* always call me to confirm these appointments of ours?"

Dr. Herman has muddy gray eyes. I've seen cats with eyes that color, but rarely humans. Like a cat's, his eyes never give away his thoughts. I'm sure he's thinking something. I want to know if he's figured out what I'm accusing him and my father of. They're both counterfeit, and hell, maybe I am too.

After a moment, he breaks eye contact with me and twists in the chair to look over his shoulder at the date book on his desk. "Our time is up. How about we continue down this road next week?"

"Sure," I mutter and leap to my feet. I get out of there as fast as I can.

———

TALKING ABOUT MY PARENTS MAKES ME PHYSICALLY ill. First, my breathing becomes hindered, and then my head sits heavy on my shoulders. For the most part, only crawling under a rock will relieve the symptoms. It's sunset, and the cold Cleveland air helps me recover. The picture of my mother with her perfectly blunt haircut, not one gray hair in her deep brunette mane, and waif-like build is dissolving from the forefront of my mind. Along with the image of Charles pushing the lawnmower on a scorching hot day, his fine, flaxen hair and matte-white skin un-scorched by the heat of the California sun.

Snow is falling, and it's the first snow of winter. I live in the city because I choose to walk wherever I need to go, no matter what the weather. At the moment, my feet beat against three inches of fallen snow. I'm heading up Prospect Avenue toward the Warehouse District. It's where I live and work, both in the same building. Regardless of the loss of traction on the roads, there's a lot of traffic. It's New

Year's Eve, so everyone is hustling and bustling to get home and prepare for the night's festivities. I pulled a midnight-to-sunrise shift at the diner this morning, but I agreed to cover for Yvette from seven until two o'clock in the morning. The shift starts in fifteen minutes. I'm never late and don't expect to be today. Yvette darn near hugged the breath out of me when I agreed to take her shift, since New Year's Eve and the Fourth of July are the only holidays I ever take off.

Usually on New Year's Eve, I fly out to one of Aries's blowout bonanzas. That's what I call them. They're over-the-top parties that, regardless of the pomp and circumstance, always turn out to be a great wholesome time. Aries, my best friend, usually throws them somewhere far away, like Cannes, or Monaco, or Amsterdam, Berlin, or Barcelona. This year, her party is in Cleveland, and I'm not in the mood to attend. Maybe the moon has shifted or my star has fallen or something, but I've been so depressed lately. For two months, I've been feeling a nudge at my brain telling me to open my eyes and resist the bubble. Aries and her parties with all her gorgeous friends are also inside the bubble.

When I reach my building on 6th Street, I rush through the lobby and up the stairs to the eighth floor. I only take the elevator if I'm carrying groceries or a pie or something. Generally, my feet are faster. Plus, I'm one of those people who have to keep moving. I feel stagnant if I stand still in an elevator for even ten seconds. As I gallop down the hallway, counting the minutes I have left to enter my apartment, change into the little pink uniform worn by waitresses everywhere, and run downstairs to the cafe, I see *him* in the stairwell. It's the guy who moved in across the hall from me two months ago.

He turns to look at me for a split second, and I stop in my tracks. I don't start walking again until he's out of sight. I have no idea why the sight of him caused my feet to stop moving. Well, actually, I do. We collided into each other on the day he moved in. I smashed my forehead against his nose so hard, I was surprised it didn't break.

Time had threatened to make me late for work that night. I rushed out the door and *wham*. It felt as if he were standing right outside of my door, waiting for the impact.

"Sorry," I said, searching for blood around his nostrils because that's how hard I'd hit him.

But there had been no blood. He hadn't even cupped his nose to indicate that it stung, which it should've. Instead, he stood firm while his eyes penetrated my soul; at least, it had felt that way. That could be because of one strange coincidence.

My eyes would be clear, like crystal clear, if it weren't for the tiny amount of gray in them. I call them pale gray, although they're much lighter than that. Kids teased me about them from grade school all the way to junior high. They called me "Ghoul Eyes" and "Ghost Eyes" and the "Eerie-eyed Girl." Even my teachers seemed leery of me.

However, some kids wanted to do more than just tease me. Once when we were walking in a single-file line returning to the classroom after recess, a girl named Lily Harper pushed me in the back. I flew forward and hit the white, dusty floor. When I twisted around to glare at her, she turned as red as a turnip. Then she rubbed her skin, crying that she was hot, that she was burning. As soon as I realized it was me doing that to her, I told myself to stop. All of a sudden, the red left her skin. She ran to the teacher, crying and scared as heck of me.

Since we stood at the end of the line, not many other classmates saw what had happened, but she was the biggest bully in school, and she had become afraid of me. I didn't have to deal with physical abuse from that day forward, but because I looked so strange, other kids mainly ignored me.

That all changed in junior high. I was thirteen, and one day, Jessie Lane, the cutest boy at school, said in front of our entire history class that I had awesome eyes. The way he said it was like he was mesmerized by them, by me. That new reaction to my peculiar eyes and my face as a whole continued into high school and through college.

But the guy across the hallway from me, our eyes are similar. I think he had noticed the resemblance as well, because we'd stared at each other for a long time after I hit him. I'd felt as though I was floating, and I saw stars or something. It was weird. And then I wondered if *his* eyes could do what mine could.

"No, *I'm* sorry," the neighbor had replied.

All I could do was gulp and gawk at him. I was pathetic. I noticed the narrow, chiseled shape of his face, his rosy lips, and his windblown hair. He'd reminded me of a world traveler, just passing through after spending a solid year skiing in the Alps. He was, and is, the physical embodiment of a breath of fresh air. We had smiled at each other on that day two months ago. Then he'd excused himself and went into his apartment. I haven't seen him since then, not until now.

I shake off the shock of running into Mister Mysterious and finish my dash to the diner on the first floor. The bells on the door handle ring as I rush in from the lobby.

Yvette is sitting on a stool at the counter, shaking her foot anxiously. She's already wearing a heavy coat and clutching her bag in her lap. "There you are!" she says, relieved.

"I'm not late," I say in my defense.

"I know, I just need to clock out sooner rather than later. Big date. Blind date." She wiggles her eyebrows dramatically as she breezes past me. "And he's cute."

I grab an order pad from behind the counter, tearing off the used ticket from a canceled order. "I thought it was a blind date?"

She pushes the door open with her back, grinning. "It is, but I had him checked out!"

I shake my head, smiling. "So, you cheated."

"I'm sure he did too. These days, time's as precious as money—none of it should go to waste."

We both laugh at that. "So, is he husband material?"

"At least on the outside. Time to lick the lollipop and see what's on the inside."

I laugh. "Well, if he checks all your boxes, I'm sure you'll check his too."

"Oh, how sweet," she sings. "See, that's another reason I hired you."

We both chuckle. She loves to tease me about why she hired me, always claiming I hypnotized her with my eyes.

Yvette's hair and skin have the rich tone of orange spice, her hazel eyes framed by brown freckles dotting her cheeks and nose. She's striking, with a look as unique as mine. Three years ago, when I first walked in asking about a job, she stared into my eyes and hired me on the spot. Then she asked if I could start in two hours.

I hesitated. I'd had no waitressing experience and wasn't even sure I wanted the job. I had just moved into the building, and after two hours of sitting alone in my apartment, I remembered the diner downstairs. The idea of working there popped into my head, but I never imagined that after casually asking if they were hiring, Yvette would immediately say, "You're hired!" She handed me a couple of uniforms, a W-4 form, and a warm hug, welcoming me to the team.

When I showed up two hours later for my first shift, Manny, the owner—short legs, round head and belly, basically a human snowman—looked at me and asked, "Who are you?"

"The new waitress," I'd replied.

He scrunched up one side of his face, studying me like he was trying to figure out when in the world he'd hired me. Later, he admitted that, in his words, "you girls are always coming and going," so it took him a minute to place me.

"The girl with the red hair hired me," I'd said, hoping to jog his memory.

"Who, Yvette?" he'd practically shouted. "What the hell! Yvette!" he called over his shoulder, his voice booming through the diner.

I remember my eyes going wide with confusion. I wasn't sure if I should stay or make a run for it. But Yvette wasn't around, and Manny clearly needed the help, so after a long sigh, he'd shaken his head and told me to get to work.

I fumbled through the first couple of days, but it didn't take long to get the hang of it.

Now, I'm the go-to girl. I've worked every Christmas Eve, Thanksgiving, and Easter since I started. Whenever one of the other girls needs a shift covered, I'm the one to ask.

"All right, Glo," Yvette says with a wave as she heads out the door.

I wave back, watching her disappear up the sidewalk. Once she's out of sight, I take a glance around the diner. I'm geared up for a long, busy shift, but there are only three customers, and they've all been served. Usually, we're packed at this time of night.

"Glo," Manny calls from behind me.

When I turn around, Manny's at the register, looking nothing like he's ready to serve the usual rowdy, celebratory New Year's Eve crowd. He's wearing shiny black slacks, a spotless white T-shirt, and a cloud of cheap cologne surrounds him. His smooth caramel skin gleams, and his jet-black wavy hair is slicked with gel.

"Hey, Manny, looking sharp," I say, heading over to the counter to grab spray cleaner and a towel. If there's no one to serve, I might as well clean.

"Yeah, yeah, yeah," he replies dismissively, punching buttons on the register. Compliments aren't his thing.

"We're closing in twenty," he says flatly.

I stop mid-wipe. "What?"

He pauses his bill counting, glancing at me, surprised by my reaction.

"It's New Year's Eve; we're closing," he grunts.

"But we've never closed before," I whine. "I can close shop by myself if that's what you're worried about."

"I thought you girls would be happy about this," he says, keeping his eyes on the credit card receipts he's stacking.

"But I…"

"You're what, twenty-one? Don't you have a party or somewhere to go to?"

"No, I'm not twenty-one," I grumble.

He grunts and looks up to study my face. "How old are you, eighteen? Because you can't work here if you are. We sell beer, and I don't want no problems."

I roll my eyes. He's always protecting his interests, even if it means reinventing the law. "I'm forty-three, Manny. Golly, don't you even check the records?"

"Get the hell out of here!" he roars.

The two guys sitting at the table by the window look over. They've been done eating since I walked in, and I notice that every now and then, one or both of them checks me out.

I put my attention back on Manny. "It's true. You want to see my ID?" I'm used to defending my age, and it's never been a compliment.

"When's your next shift?"

I lift my eyebrows, astonished. "You think I'm lying?"

"If you're saying you're forty-three, you are." He pokes himself in the chest. "I'm forty." He points at me. "You're a kid."

I grunt and shake my head. "Thursday's my next shift. I have to cover for Melissa."

He points at me again. "No, you don't. Stop letting those goddamn girls take advantage of you. You're too nice. You need to find your inside bitch." He slams the drawer shut. "I'll bring my wife over. She'll give you lessons. For free. Now lock the front door and flip the sign. They'll go out the side when they're done."

"But—" I start but then think better about whining and just do as I'm told.

He's not going to change his mind. Plus, he believes he's doing me a favor. If I didn't live in the bubble, then being off tonight would be all roses.

I think I muttered a quick "Whatever" as I stomped off to check on the two guys who, I knew for sure, lived in the building. One of them casually asked for my number and invited me out for the night. I assured him there'd be no New Year's Eve hoopla for me.

Now, standing in my robe and gazing out the floor-to-ceiling windows of my apartment, I watch partygoers trudge up and down 6th Street. A lukewarm glass of cabernet sauvignon in hand, I'm hoping two glasses will lull me to sleep. Lately, though, my mind can't seem to stop racing when I lie down. I'm restless, even now, and for reasons I still can't quite figure out.

As I sip my wine, my cell phone rings, and I rush to check the caller ID. A sigh escapes me, heavy with the weight of what I'm about to do.

"Hi, Aries," I answer, trying to sound as pleasant as possible. Over the years, I've trained myself to respond only with emotions that keep me agreeable. Manny was right—I have no "inside" bitch. I haven't since elementary school, when I scared Lily Harper—and myself—by putting fire to her.

"I heard you didn't have to work tonight," Aries practically shouts into my ear. I can hear slow, steady music thumping in the background, so I pull the phone away just a bit.

"Who told you that?" I ask, genuinely curious. How could she know?

"What?" she yells again.

I bring the phone closer to my mouth. "Who told you I don't have to work tonight?"

"Someone."

"Who's someone?"

She sighs, clearly annoyed. "Who the hell cares, Glo? Get yourself down here!"

I shake my head, feeling that familiar frustration rise. Aries always seems to know too much. Like the time she knew I got the job at the diner before I even told her. Or ten years ago, when she was the first person I called after my parents were killed in a car accident. She didn't even let me get the words out before she asked, "How are you holding up?"

I'd thought maybe she had heard the news from one of her parents, but a few days later, I realized that they couldn't have known before *me*. I had been called only hours after the accident occurred, and the police kept the details from the public until I traveled to Toledo to identify the bodies. Plus, Aries's parents still lived in California, so they couldn't have heard about the head-on collision on the local news.

Aries and I had grown up in Cerritos, California, one of Los Angeles County's many suburban cities. Our neighbors were working mothers and fathers who shopped on the weekends and dined at restaurants like Sizzler on weeknights. We were the kind of kids who hung out at the Cerritos Mall, and when we were done with the food court and the boys there, we'd take the city bus over to the Lakewood Mall, on the opposite side of the 605 Freeway, just to change it up a bit.

I met Aries one late afternoon on the bus heading back to my side of town. I had just ditched the two girls I used to hang out with every now and then, Tabatha and Lacy. They were the kind of girls who got hot for every cute boy who paid them some attention. We had met these three boys in Metallica T-shirts with ripped sleeves and tapered black khaki shorts with chains linking the front pocket to the back pocket. The boys were really busy trying to convince us to go over to their house and *hang*. Their shiny red apple was *Donkey Kong* and a swimming pool. My two counterparts needed no arm-twisting to take a bite, but I wasn't interested.

"Come on, come over," one of the guys begged

me. "My buddy really likes you. Unless you like me, then I like you." He flashed a sincere smile after making that proclamation.

He *was* cute, and we were the same height, which was good. I was 5'11" even back then. The problem stemmed from me being afraid—but not of the boys. See, they might not have liked me so much if they had known I could hurt them with the eyes they found so enthralling. If they knew what I could do to them if something happened to go wrong, they would have run as far away from me as possible—even Tabatha and Lacy would. So I said good-bye and left them all standing there, watching me walk away.

That was the last time I'd ever spoken to those two girls. From that day forward, they would just whisper to each other and roll their eyes whenever they saw me. I don't know what happened after I left, but in their minds, I was the one to blame for it. But it didn't matter. Leaving them had allowed me to keep my appointment with destiny.

I later met Aries, the bus had stopped and opened its door just as I was passing the stop. I could walk home faster than the bus could carry me, so I don't know what prompted me to get on board, but I made a snap decision to take the ride up South Street.

After I'd settled in a seat, I saw that there was this crazy guy onboard who'd convinced himself that he was Michael Jackson, the Prince of Pop. I mean, that's what he called himself. "Michael Jackson, the Prince of Pop." The girl sitting across from me and I couldn't stop giggling as he moonwalked up and down the aisle, singing a nasally version of "Billie Jean." Then she clapped and sang along, which did nothing but add fuel to his fire. He really started putting on a show then! He would go from the front of the bus where he'd kick up a knee, swing his leg, and cry, "Ugh," in a high-pitched tone, and then repeat that at the back of the bus.

He wore black jeans that were rolled up to expose his ankles, a red fake leather jacket with half the glass studs missing, and one white satin glove on his left hand. But he didn't stop there. He wore thick black eyeliner, white powder instead of foundation on his face, and bright red blush on each of his cheeks. At one point I found myself wondering who he really was. Even though he gave quite a fun performance, I wanted to know where he slept at night.

However, the bus driver wasn't as entertained as

we were. He kept shouting, "Sit down, sir," over the intercom.

Strangely enough, the driver was quite patient until Mr. MJ Impersonator grabbed his crotch right in front of the driver's face. That's when the bus had come to a screeching halt, and we heard the driver curse under his breath as he pressed buttons to call the police. Of course, Mr. Michael Jackson Wannabe high-tailed it out of there, cursing at the driver for being ungrateful as he escaped.

Aries and I couldn't stop laughing. When anyone asks how we met, our answer is always at a concert Michael Jackson gave on a city bus. That was the day we became friends, and I learned she lived around the block from me, which made it all the better.

We were fifteen years old then. And here's the clincher—I know I'm a freak of nature. Anyone who can make things hot just by looking at them or see through doors and walls obviously has some serious issues. But Aries, like me, hasn't aged a day. She still looks exactly the same as she did twenty-five years ago. That, too, seems bizarre.

I mean, looking young forever doesn't quite compare to being able to see through steel or start fires with your eyes, but it's strange in its own way.

Yet, I can't shake this feeling that Aries and my parents are cut from the same stone—the same stone that gave me these abilities. I know how crazy that sounds, and maybe it is.

That's why her knowing I'm off work, just minutes after the diner closed, feels off. And the fact that she mentioned it so casually makes me wonder if she secretly wants me to dig deeper, to finally press her for the truth. But I always stop myself. I think, deep down, I don't really want to know. Avoidance—that's what my parents taught. Keep the peace, even if it means turning a blind eye to the truth.

So, I let it slide. I don't confront her with my suspicions. A lot of her friends live in the Warehouse District. She knows half my building and three-quarters of Cleveland, and probably most people in other major cities, too. That's another thing about Aries—she's incredibly social. It makes me doubt my suspicions sometimes. Someone with so many "normal" friends has to be normal too, right?

"Well…" The wine is doing its job, and I feel completely at ease. "I'm staying in tonight."

"No, you're not," she counters, her voice firm.

"It's New Year's Eve, and I'm hosting the party in Cleveland this year. You know that."

"Yes, I know," I admit, knowing where this is heading.

"You know?" She exaggerates her shock. "You *know*!"

"All right, all right, I get it." I roll my eyes, trying to fend off the guilt trip.

"I can't believe I have to convince you," she huffs. "Everyone who's anyone wants to be here, but I've got to twist *my best friend's* arm? Glo, that's not a good look."

I let out another long, heavy sigh. "Okay..." My tone clearly shows how unenthusiastic I am about the decision.

"So get your butt down here, beautiful, or I'm coming to get you. And you know I will," Aries warns.

I picture her at my door, rifling through my closet, standing over me, insisting I apply makeup the way she wants—always ending with me in a chalky mess of gray and black eyeshadow. She calls it smoky eyes. I call it creepy eyes.

"Okay, just give me the address," I grumble.

"Didn't you get the invitation?"

I roll my eyes. "I did, but..."

"You lost it? Threw it away? Shame on you," she teases, adding the signature Aries giggle before rattling off the address. Then, she hangs up.

I LIVE IN A TWO-BEDROOM FLAT, ONLY BECAUSE THE one-bedroom I wanted wasn't available. My place is almost empty, but that's how I prefer it. I'm a mini-malist—everything has its place, and I like it clean and simple. In my living room, I have just a red microfiber chair and a matching sofa, with a flat-screen TV mounted above the fireplace. There's a glass coffee table between them, mostly because it completes the standard "living room" setup. That's it. Each bedroom has nothing more than a bed and a dresser. It's how I like my space—and my life—clean, uncluttered, and straightforward.

Since it's snowing tonight, I pull on a thick red turtleneck sweater dress that I'd ordered from the Victoria's Secret catalog. Three-quarters of my wardrobe comes from there—it's easy, and every-thing fits my figure and height perfectly. I add a pair of black fishnet stockings and slip into black furry snow boots with a slight heel to give my outfit a dressed-up touch for the occasion.

As I stand in front of the bathroom mirror applying mascara, my thoughts drift to my neighbor. Did he really look at me earlier when I passed him in the hallway? Fantasizing about him already has me at a disadvantage. No one ever truly gets their fantasies fulfilled, right? It's not like I'm imagining anything inappropriate—just replaying the moment we first met.

In my mind, we're locked in each other's gaze, and my head feels like it's floating, a sensation better than sex. In my version of the moment, he asks my name.

"Glo," I whisper.

"Beautiful," he whispers back.

No one has ever called my three-letter name "beautiful." In elementary school, the kids used to call me "Flo," like the character from *Alice*, that old TV show about waitresses at Mel's Diner. They'd tease me with that nasally Southern drawl, "Kiss my grits." After the incident with Lily, though, they stopped saying it to my face. It's funny how now that I actually work in a diner, I never hear that joke anymore.

In my fantasy, after my neighbor compliments my name, we continue gazing into each other's eyes. I'm waiting for him to ask me out—or say something. He never does, and that's where my daydream fades out.

As I wonder what he's doing right at this very moment, I aim my gaze toward the walk-in shower, peering past the spotless glass door. My thoughts linger on the edge of temptation, flirting with the idea of seeing through the mustard-colored ceramic tile. My breath becomes unsteady as I weigh the choice. I glance over both shoulders as if someone might catch me in the act. But there's no one—except God as a witness.

I refocus on the tile. Step by step, I let my eyes work their magic. The hallway appears, empty as expected. Just one more wall to see through. My conscience nags at me, warning not to invade a stranger's privacy, but I silence it. I press on, commanding my eyes to pierce through the white plaster and wooden beams.

Suddenly, my eyes widen. My breath hitches for a count of two. To my utter shock, he meets my gaze. I gasp, yanking myself back, staring at my own reflection in disbelief.

Was he looking back at me?

I STOP BREATHING FOR WHAT FEELS LIKE AN eternity as I make my way down the hallway, something that's oddly easy to do. So far, the mysterious neighbor is still inside his apartment.

Did we just lock eyes?

No, it couldn't be. It must've been a coincidence.

I hit the stairwell, and my boots clunk, clunk, clunk down each metal step. When I finally step outside and trot up St. Clair Avenue, I can't shake the feeling that someone is following me. I glance over my shoulder, but it's just the usual crowd—people in party mode, sidewalks buzzing with life, cars honking. It's New Year's Eve, after all. Every bar and club is packed, but I know they'll all close by two a.m.

That's why Aries never goes to them. She says if you can't party from sundown to sunup, you might as well stay home and paint your toenails. She's the kind of woman who'll hop on a private jet at any moment just to chase wherever the party lasts past two.

But this is Cleveland, not New York City. I've always thought her lifestyle would be more fitting in a place like Manhattan, where everything moves as fast as she does. Every time I ask Aries if she stays here because of me, she denies it, and vehemently so. She's an investment banker for the Cork Group, with offices downtown but headquartered in Manhattan. She's always jetting off for work, traveling to cities all over the world. Yet, no matter how far she goes, she's never gone for more than three or four days at a time. She always makes it back in time to go grocery shopping with me, or grab lunch, coffee, or dinner, like clockwork.

It's just so strange that she is always around, effortlessly weaving herself into my life. I'm not complaining. She's the perfect friend. We've never had a falling out, not once. She always knows what to say. I love it when she calls to tell me to switch to a random TV channel to watch some kid sing their heart out, hoping to be famous. She's obsessed with those competition shows—singing, dancing, cooking, you name it. That's pretty much all she watches whenever she has time for TV.

And that's my friend. I love her, truly, which is why I'm standing here now, in front of this towering skyscraper on Rockwell Avenue, about to head into her New Year's Eve party.

The towering height of the building confirms she wasn't joking when she said the thirty-third floor. The ground floor is buzzing with luxury, from doormen to valet parking attendants, all suited up in thick black coats over their sharp black suits. Sleek cars pull up to the booths, and the men leave their heated canopies to hurry over and open doors for the drivers and their guests.

It's clear the partygoers here are from some-where upscale. They look like they stepped out of a Grey Goose vodka commercial, sleek and sophisti-cated, primed for a night of indulgence. Their eyes are wide, alive with anticipation, eager to escape the snow and head up to the thirty-third floor where the real action awaits.

These are Aries's people—she knows every single one of them personally. The only "friend" we both share is Raz, her long-time boyfriend. And oddly enough, just like Aries, he hasn't aged a day.

As I take the steps up to the doors, a multi-colored light and smoke effect flows across my legs. This imaginative touch makes the gorgeous faces around me even more eager to get to our final desti-nation. Shielding us from the snow flurries is a canopy extending from the sidewalk all the way to the glass doors. There are even patio heaters posi-tioned along the steps to keep us warm. Aries always thinks of these small details.

As I make my way toward the back of the

surprisingly short line, one of the two burly men in black suits, clipboard in hand, suddenly calls out, "Glo Slater," and waves me over.

All eyes immediately land on me, scanning me from head to toe. None of the other women would dare show up to a party like this in a sweater dress from a catalog. Their looks are heavy with judgment, but I don't care. I've never been the slinky dress type, and that's fine by me.

"Have a ball, sexy," the doorman purrs, giving me a very obvious once-over. He's definitely flirting.

I offer a polite smile as I slip past him, check my coat, and take my ticket. In the elevator, two women in perfectly tailored black cocktail dresses stand with a couple, all of them sneaking glances at me. I don't acknowledge them. I know I stand out here. In a room full of glamour, I'm always the odd one out— with my strange looks and long, spiraling auburn hair that refuses to blend in.

I used to cut my hair every three days to keep it at neck length. If I shave it off, it grows back to this length in seven days, tops. During my freshman year of college, I went through a phase where I took clippers to it every day. The look suited me—like a fierce, reptilian Amazon warrior, à la Sinead O'Connor. Aries and I eventually chalked it up to some genetic quirk. As long as it didn't spread across my whole body and turn me into Bigfoot or Chewbacca, we figured there was no point in worrying. And mostly, I don't.

In the elevator, the two women in black dresses start whispering in French. My French isn't great, but I can catch the gist. One of them says, "Aries's friend."

The other says, "*Je vois*," and then, "*modéle?*"

"*J'imagine*," the first one answers.

They always assume I'm a model, as if I have the patience to be poked, prodded, and paraded down a runway in overpriced, uncomfortable clothes. There's no way I can endure that.

I exhale in relief as the elevator doors slide open; I hate when strangers talk about me. I let everyone exit first, except for the man who, sensing my discomfort, politely steps aside for the women to pass. I raise a hand, shaking my head, fighting back an unexpected urge to cry. He seems to sense it too and quickly makes his exit.

"Get a grip," I whisper to myself. My emotions have been all over the place lately. I can go from feeling perfectly happy to deeply sad in the span of a heartbeat. It's the anxiety, constantly lurking just beneath the surface, keeping me on edge. I can feel a change coming, like I'm standing on the precipice of something—I just can't quite see what it is.

But I reach for the part of me that says she's going to have a good time tonight, here in the bubble. I stick my hand between the doors before they close, and they open again. I take a deep breath and walk out of the elevator and into the celebration.

———

THE ENTIRE FLOOR IS WIDE OPEN, AND PEOPLE ARE everywhere. Sensual music flows into my ears. The lighting is dim blue and silver. The sadness that had affected me a few seconds ago gives way to anticipation.

I slip past the groups of bodies holding three-quarters-filled champagne and cocktail glasses. People seem to be having a good time; they're laughing and gesturing and dancing—lots and lots of dancing. As far as I can see, not one person is bored.

Two guys in dark, crisp, loose-fitting jeans and spotless white T-shirts take the stage that's strategically placed in the middle of the room. The crowd goes crazy. I don't recognize the performers, but from all the whistling, clapping, and catcalling, they must be popular. It wouldn't be an Aries Johnson throw-down hoedown without big names taking the stage.

"Yeah, yeah," the guys start in the way all rappers speak before their performance.

The partygoers erupt in more applause as a rock instrument starts up. I take a second look at the entertainers. I thought they were singing rap, but I guess not. They've scratched my curiosity, and I'm eager to hear more when I feel a tap on my shoulder. I turn around.

"You made it," Aries sings with her arms open wide.

We hug as the guys on stage go into the sort of song that makes me want to let loose and dance.

"I did," I shout above the music, my eyes scanning the room.

"You look…"—she holds my arms out to get an eyeful of me—"warm!"

I laugh. "That's because I am!"

She scrunches up her face and touches one of her ears. "Come on! It's quieter in the atrium!"

Aries takes my hand and leads me along. She looks stunning in a skin-kissing, slinky powder-blue dress that contrasts with gorgeous chocolate skin.

She's the same color as a Hershey's Kiss. We tested it one night when we were sixteen and having one of our million sleepovers. She has jet-black hair that she wears thick and wild these days. I can't even capture in words what a stunning creature she is.

She's hugging, double-kissing, and squeezing the hands of partygoers as we go, promising to "talk later." And she will. Later, she'll go up to each and every one of them, touch their arm or shoulder, and ask the right question. Each person will feel like they've had an hour-long conversation with her about something very amusing. Aries isn't one of those fake people who say things in the moment to make people like her. She's an expert at spreading happiness.

Our feet bounce up a spiraling metal stairwell. The music follows us until we enter a glass-covered rooftop patio. People are lounging on red velour couches around fire-pits. They're taking drags on their cigarettes or swallowing healthy doses of the drinks in their glasses, having a good time.

At one pit, everyone's watching a guy follow a metal medallion on a string with his eyes. They're watching him close, waiting for him to miss.

"You're a sable, Javi," Aries calls over her shoulder. She slides over to one of the pits where Raz, her very cute boyfriend, is already seated.

"Glo!" he sings, as if the sight of me has just made his night. He gets up and leans over to give me a gigantic hug.

"Raz, you look… the same!"

And he does. He looks just as he did the day I met him at some remote beach up Pacific Coast Highway. Aries had wanted to introduce me to her boyfriend, so we drove from Cerritos to Pacific Coast Highway in her Pontiac Grand Am. We kept going north past Santa Monica's and Malibu's popular beach hangouts. When there was nothing but hills to the east of us and trees to the west, she cut a U-turn and parked along the side of the road. From there, we had a twenty-minute walk up rocky paths. We crawled down slippery mountainsides and sloshed through thick sand. I kept picturing Raz as a guy who looked like Schleprock with a surfboard, because any person who would go through all of that to do nothing but surf had to be a cartoon character slash beach bum.

But he wasn't Schleprock. He was gorgeous and well put-together with clichéd California-boy looks: shaggy blond hair, blue eyes, sun-tanned skin, no shirt, muscular chest, and he spoke with a drag. He greeted me as if he'd known me forever, and since I felt the same way, I responded in the same manner. I swear that I'm looking at that same boy now.

"You're beautiful as ever," Raz says as he drops back down onto the couch.

Aries scoots toward him, and when she gets close enough, he draws her into him with one arm. Others are sitting around the fire, eyeing me and wondering who I am. There are three guys, all super-attractive of course, and four other good-looking women.

"So this is Seb, Kim, Aya, Kefir, Upton, Blythe, and Nina, and this is Glo," Aries says as I sit down next to her.

"Hi," I say while waving coyly.

Each person responds with a tight-lipped smile. One of them, maybe Upton, lifts a hand and gives me *the eyes*. Really, I do *not* expect much warmth from this crowd. Others would consider them rude, but to me, their behavior couldn't be more welcoming.

"So we were on our way to Milan when it happened," one of the girls says. It sounds like she's finishing a conversation.

"But Raz has a story that tops that," Kefir says.

He has an Aussie accent. "Tell them about riding the monkey, bro."

They all break out into laughter.

Aries takes my hand. "I'm so glad you came," she says in my ear.

"You said that already." I smile.

"Well, it's not easy to convince you to come out and have fun when you decide you'd rather stay in and sulk all night."

"I don't *sulk*."

"Yeah, you do." She flips her hand dismissively. "But that's neither here nor there."

I shake my head because deep down, I know she's right. "Well, I'm here, and I'm ready to have fun," I sing with a cynical tone.

Aries puts her smoldering eyes on the guy named Upton. "Isn't he cute?" she whispers in my ear.

I observe him. He notices and smiles at me. I look away in a hurry.

"He can't keep his eyes off of you," she purrs.

"He is kind of my type," I whisper.

"Kind of is." She shifts to face me fully.

I know what that means. Our discussion of the cute guy across the fire-pit has ceased. Now it's up to me to go get him or not.

"I'm still happy to see you tonight," she simpers, looping her arm through mine. "What's been going on with you anyways? I've been in Maui all week."

My mind betrays me and flashes a picture of the neighbor across the hall. When I look into Aries's eyes, I swear she sees it too. For a fraction of a second, while his image appears in my head, the sides of her mouth turn down.

"Work," I reply.

She grunts with a hint of suspicion. "That's it, huh?"

"Other than the session with my shrink, that's it."

"Oh, how's that going?"

"The same."

She shakes her head. "What does that mean? Gosh, Glo, talking to you is like pulling teeth. I tell *you* everything."

"*This* is what we talked about last week."

"I'm officially confused."

"You're making me feel guilty, and you do it deliberately."

She throws one arm around my neck. "That's because I love you, and I know what's best for you, way better than what you know for yourself some-times." She giggles.

Now, I'm beaming. That's what I mean. She knows how to defuse any argument between us with the right words or gestures, which always involves a touch of some sort.

"But really, is Dr. Herman helping with… you know?" she asks.

Ding, the alarm sounds again. I mean, who remembers the name of their friend's shrink? I rarely mention his name. *Rarely*. "Not really."

She's referring to my parents' death. I started seeing him right after they died because I felt really lost. Not because I was brokenhearted and had no direction in my life, but because I didn't believe it. Even after seeing their charred bodies, I didn't believe they were dead. They were never real, so how could they be dead?

"Then why are you still seeing him?" she asks.

"I have no idea; I think I'll stop though."

"You should. You don't need psychotherapy. You never did."

I frown. "You're the one who said I should get some help." Yes, I'm one-hundred-percent sure she's the one who suggested it.

"I meant with packing up of all your parents' things, selling the house, and so forth. That kind of help!"

I take a moment to ponder what she just said. I'm more confused than ever! "How did you conclude that I needed help with tasks from, 'I think I need to talk to someone?'" I shake my head in defiance. I won't let her chalk up her suggesting I get a little psychotherapy to a misunderstanding. "No, Aries, you absolutely *knew* what I meant, but now you're pretending you didn't. Why?"

"I seriously don't remember, Glo-light, but if you say so... If I thought you needed a shrink *then*, I'm absolutely sure you don't need one *now*."

My mouth falls open. How can I argue with her *now*? Back her into a corner and get her to confess? Confess what? I just know there's something. By the look on her face, she's waiting for me to apologize for snapping at her like I usually do.

"Hey, babe, let's dance," Raz says after laughing at what one of the guys said. They were all talking about a waterfall that Raz and a few buddies canoed down and were fortunate to live to tell the tale.

Raz takes her hand as he stands, but Aries remains seated, looking into my eyes. Gosh, the guilt trip. Yes, I feel guilty; I can't help it.

"I'm sorry," I whisper and touch her arm. "Go dance."

She nods stiffly. "I'm sorry too. I didn't mean to get you upset. I love you, you know that."

"I know," I say, still wondering what just happened. Why am I right back at square one? Why can't Aries assure me just once that if there's a bubble, then she knows nothing about it?

Aries and Raz go skipping off downstairs. The others, who are eager to please the hosts, follow, leaving me alone with Upton. I know he's been waiting for a moment alone with me.

"Hi," he says, lifting a hand.

I put on a smile. "Hi."

He's wearing yellow pants and a gold lamé button-down, long-sleeved shirt. The outfit isn't hideous. From the richness of the material, I'd say his apparel cost him a pretty penny. I just wonder if he's one-hundred-percent straight. If he's American, then he's not.

"I see you know Aries quite well," he says with an accent. He's not American; there's a strong possibility he's straight.

I'm not a prude, and he's cute. I like guys. Cute guys. Being good-looking is half the battle. The other half is keeping me interested.

"Yes, we're good friends," I say.

"May I?" He points to the empty space beside me.

I shrug. "Sure."

His cologne isn't off-putting, and neither is his smile. He has really bold white teeth. He stares right into my eyes. "You're bloody breathtaking. Are you a model of some sorts?"

"No. I'm a waitress."

"Is that right? You should model. I actually know some people."

"Me too," I assure him.

He lifts one side of his mouth into a lopsided smile. "I'm quite sure you do."

"You're English?" I ask.

"Why yes, how could you tell?" He grins.

I laugh lightly, appreciatively. I love sarcasm. "Well, Upton, do you dance?"

"Only when necessary," he replies.

"Oh, it's necessary."

We've somehow moved our faces closer together. He's on the verge of answering when I feel a hand on my left shoulder. I look up and, lo and behold, to my utter shock, it's my neighbor.

CHAPTER 2

MEET THE NEIGHBOR

"It's you," I manage to say, my throat tight with emotion.

He isn't smiling. In fact, his expression is the opposite—hard, unreadable. "We need to talk," he says, his eyes narrowing as they shift to Upton.

Upton, sensing the tension, glances between us, his eyebrows lifting as if something suddenly clicks in his mind. "Right," he says, hopping to his feet with newfound urgency. "Very well then, I'll let you two talk. I'll just, uh, scurry downstairs. Join me when you're finished?"

I stand up, mirroring Upton's stance. "Sure, I'll find you when we're done."

The neighbor and I watch Upton disappear into

the stairwell. Once he's out of sight, I waste no time.

"Why are you here?" I ask before he even looks at me.

He turns, his eyes sharp. "Who are you?"

"I'm Glo Decker. Who are you?"

He ignores my question, his gaze unwavering. "You saw me, didn't you?"

I blink, caught off guard by his bluntness. "You saw me too?"

"I did."

I almost choke, caught off guard by his directness. Especially about something so... impossible. "So I guess the real question is, why can we both see each other?"

"Do you know why?" he asks, his intensity unyielding.

This guy is all business—no smile, no charm, just a demanding presence. It's unsettling, but I'm too curious to back down.

"I don't," I admit, disappointment leaking into my tone.

"You're able to go outside in the daylight, aren't you?" he asks.

I frown, thrown by the strangeness of his question. "Am I able to go outside in the daylight? Of course. Aren't you?"

He shakes his head, his expression turning sour like he's biting into lemons. "Are you human?"

I slap my chest in disbelief, my voice faltering. "I…" The words stick in my throat, and suddenly, I'm unsure. Why do I feel like the answer might not be what I want it to be?

Suddenly, he stiffens, snapping his head toward the stairwell. His entire demeanor shifts. "I have to go," he mutters, turning those unnervingly clear eyes, which mirror my own, back to me one last time before darting away.

I stand there, unnerved, feeling like I've just stared into a mirror. My blinks are slow, my breaths heavy, as if something unseen is pulling at me. I've heard a woman can fall under a man's spell if she looks at him a second too long, and I think that's what's happening now.

"Who were you talking to?" Aries asks, her voice cutting through the music and chatter like a bell.

I jump, startled, whipping around to see her approaching with a crimped brow, her gaze sweeping over the patio. There's something protective, almost menacing, in her expression that unsettles me. But it's her question that really throws me off. Aries couldn't have seen me talking to my neighbor unless she, like me, could see through walls.

"Did you see me talking to someone?" I challenge, keeping my voice casual.

Her smile turns sweet, like spun sugar. "Oh, I saw Upton downstairs. He mentioned you were with some guy."

"Really? I wonder why he said that." I feign ignorance, playing dumb.

She's still scanning the area, clearly looking for my neighbor. But there's no sign of him, and with the glass roof overhead, I can't imagine how he slipped in—or out.

"Well…" She finally gives up the search and grabs my wrist, tugging me gently. "Come on, it's almost time for the countdown, and you don't want to start the New Year without a kiss." She grins mischievously. "Upton's waiting for you."

NOT A SINGLE PARTYGOER IS SITTING DOWN, AND neither am I. We're all moving, swaying to the rhythm of a sultry French song being belted out by a woman in a long red dress, her thick afro wig swaying with each note. The music is hypnotic, pulling us all into its spell.

I place my hands on Upton's shoulders, moving seductively as I dip low, then rise, curling my hips, trying to immerse myself in the moment. But no matter how much I try, I can't shake thoughts of my neighbor. His face was so close to mine, and he was here—actually here. The urge to go home, knock on his door, and finish our conversation lingers in my mind, but I force myself to stay, to pretend I'm having fun.

Aries is watching me, keeping close, her intent clear. I know she's making sure I stay engaged. Upton's arm snakes around my waist, pulling me closer. As the crowd counts down to the new year, I can't help but feel torn, lost between the present and the mystery still waiting for me at home.

The countdown begins.

"Ten!" the crowd shouts.

"I really like you," Upton whispers in my ear.

"Nine!"

"I like you too," I reply, though my neighbor lingers in the back of my mind. Still, I can make room for Upton.

"Eight, seven, six!"

"So, are we kissing?" he asks, his breath warm against my ear.

"Five, four, three!"

"Are we?" I tease back.

"Two, one—Happy New Year!" explodes all around us.

Upton presses his lips to mine for a kiss that lasts just long enough to suit the moment. I glance toward Aries out of the corner of my eye. At first, she's watching us, but soon enough, one friend after another pulls her into hugs, and she disappears into the crowd.

I see my chance and gently pull away, bringing the kiss with Upton to an end. "Give me a minute," I whisper in his ear. "I need to go to the loo."

He chuckles, amused by my use of his lingo, and releases me, though I can feel his reluctance. As I strut away, weaving through the crowd, I already know one thing for certain—I'm not coming back.

———

IIT'S SO WARM AND COZY INSIDE THAT I NEARLY forgot how freezing it is outside. The wind has picked up, and the streets are full of drunk twenty-somethings stumbling up the avenues, shouting

"Happy New Year!" and giggling as they trip over each other. It's a sloppy, carefree display, but in a few years, most of them will be settled down, and all of this will be a distant memory.

I shuffle through the snow on the un-shoveled sidewalks, the icy wind nipping at my face. My heart races in anticipation, pounding with the thought of seeing him again. He did say we'd talk later, didn't he? When I reach my building, I fumble with my keycard, my fingers clumsy from nerves and cold.

As soon as I step into the lobby, a wave of warmth hits me, both from the heat and my own anxious energy. I can't shake the conversation I had with the mysterious neighbor. I know it was real—it had to be. I take the elevator up instead of the stairs, too jittery to think about climbing.

"Get ahold of yourself," I mutter under my breath. One thing's for sure, though—the neighbor isn't interested in me romantically. That much I know. He interested in whether or not I'm a human being.

The elevator doors slide open, and I step out, my pulse quickening with each step down the hallway toward his apartment. For the first time in a long while, it feels like I'm on the verge of cracking through the invisible walls of the bubble I've lived in for so long. It's as if this neighbor holds the key to freeing me from something I didn't even realize had been holding me back.

I hesitate briefly, torn between knocking on his door or retreating to my own apartment and waiting for him to come to me. The giddiness bubbling up inside me is almost embarrassing, but I can't help it.

And then, as if answering my silent dilemma, his door swings open, almost invitingly. I know he's done it for me—he's waiting.

Without hesitation, I step inside.

HE CLOSES THE DOOR BEHIND ME, AND THE HALLWAY light disappears, plunging us into complete darkness. Strangely, I'm not nervous. There's no fear, no panic. Instead, I feel a heightened sense of everything around me, even in the absence of light.

"Where are the windows?" I ask, noticing the lack of natural light.

"I blocked them out," he replies, his voice calm, almost matter-of-fact.

A dim ceiling light flickers on, casting a faint

glow over the room. The space is nearly empty, save for two armchairs facing each other. It's even sparser than my own place. Minimalism taken to the extreme.

"You live here?" I ask, the thought crossing my mind that maybe this isn't his home after all, which would explain why I've barely seen him around.

He stands so close that I suddenly notice an icy chill radiating from him, colder than the room itself. The contrast sends a shiver through me, yet it's the intensity of his gaze—so steady and unflinching— that truly leaves me breathless.

"Sometimes," he repeats, his voice as steady as his gaze.

"Oh, is that why I never see you around? Because you 'sometimes' live here?" I ask, glancing again at the sparse, almost barren space.

"You look for me?" There's a hint of curiosity in his tone, maybe even a touch of amusement, which strikes me as odd—he doesn't seem like the humorous type.

"No, it's not that. I mean, you live right across the hall, and I hardly ever see or hear you."

His expression is so serious, so unyielding, and yet it makes my heart race wildly. But now a sliver of doubt creeps in. Maybe I *should* be afraid. No rational woman would be standing in this nearly empty, dark apartment with a man she barely knows. The place has the eerie feel of a trap, like something from a crime documentary.

Suddenly, I'm hyper-aware of the door behind me, mapping out an escape route. My eyes—my hidden power—are poised and ready, just in case his intentions turn sinister.

He reaches out, gently pressing a finger beneath my left eye. "You saw me earlier, through the walls." It's not even a question—more like a revelation. There's something almost reassuring in the way he says it.

I swallow hard, my heart pounding against my ribcage as if trying to escape. The strange mix of attraction and fear swirling between us is undeniable. "What's your name?" I manage to ask, my voice barely steady.

"Finn," he replies, his gaze locked on mine, unwavering.

"Yes," I admit, the truth spilling out easily. "I can see through walls." For the first time, saying it doesn't make me feel crazy.

"And you're human?" he asks, his voice taking on a strange intensity.

There it is again—that odd question. "I am. Aren't you?"

His expression remains unchanged as he delivers an unsettling answer. "No."

"I'm sorry," I say, blinking rapidly, my mind scrambling to catch up. "Did you just say, 'no'?"

"I did."

A snort escapes me, dripping with sarcasm. "Is this a joke?"

"No," he replies, his tone as calm and matter-of-fact as before.

I stare at him, my mind refusing to accept what he's telling me.

Yet by the look on his face, I can't help but follow this bizarre trail of revelations. "So, if you're not human, then what are you?"

"I'm a vampire."

I laugh—loud and sharp—because what else could I do? This guy has to be insane. "I'm leaving," I snap, turning on my heel.

But just as I whip around, I freeze. My mind stumbles to comprehend what just happened. Finn… he somehow appeared right in front of me, blocking my exit. My heart races, panic rising in my chest. Before I realize it, something inside me ignites.

A guttural cry tears from Finn's throat as he collapses, crumpling to the ground. I'm burning him—my eyes are scorching his flesh. He writhes, grunting, screeching in agony.

"S-s-stop," he whimpers, his voice barely audible over the pain.

Shaken, I snap my eyes shut, and immediately, the burning sensation vanishes. My breathing is ragged, and my hands are trembling. What did I just do?

He struggles to stand, ripping off his burnt shirt, smoke still snaking from the skin on his perfectly smooth chest. Oddly enough, there's no char, no blood—just unscathed, unmarred flesh. I'm relieved, but also caught in a whirlwind of emotions—amazement, confusion, and, most of all, curiosity.

"You've already answered my next question," he says, dragging himself past me to flop down into one of the chairs. His eyes close, as if the effort of recovering from the burn took more out of him than he's willing to show. "Could you please sit? I promise I won't hurt you. If I try, feel free to do what you just did again."

For some reason, despite everything that just happened, I believe him. Reluctantly, I sit down, my nerves still buzzing, ready to spring into action if I have to. But now... I want answers.

"Sorry about that," I say, my eyes still fixed on the smoke lazily rising from his skin.

"Don't worry about it."

"Does it hurt?" I ask, breaking the silence.

"You almost killed me."

"So... does that mean yes?"

For the first time, he cracks a slight smile. "Yes, that means yes."

"Oh..."

Silence falls between us again. I can tell he needs a moment to recover before continuing whatever conversation he has in mind.

"But what you did to me—it's a good thing," he finally says, surprising me.

I frown. "It is?"

"You can kill us very easily."

"Vampires?" I ask skeptically.

"You still don't believe me?" His eyes lock onto mine, filled with that same intense certainty that leaves me questioning everything I thought I knew.

I try to make sense of what he's saying, but it just seems so absurd. Vampires? That's folklore— old European tales meant to scare and control religious people, which I am certainly not. "Well... no. I don't believe you. Not at all."

He opens his mouth, touching the two fangs that rest on either side. "I wasn't born with these. They appeared when I became a vampire. They come and go depending on my mood."

"So, right now, you're in the mood for fangs?" I scoff. My cynicism surprises even me.

His eyes roam over me, slow and deliberate, like he's peeling away layers I didn't know I had. "I am," he replies, voice steady, eyes piercing. "But it doesn't matter. I can smell you, and you don't smell human."

"Really? And what exactly do I smell like?"

He narrows his eyes, like he's contemplating something far deeper than he wants to say. "I don't know."

I frown, feeling the weight of his words hit harder than expected. He's confirming everything I've feared for so long—that I'm not normal.

"You have eyes like mine," I whisper, my throat tight as if I'm finally confessing a secret I've held onto for too long. "You saw what else I can do with mine besides see through things. What else can your eyes do?"

He stands up, and I watch as he strides into the

kitchen, returning moments later with a cocktail glass in hand.

"Watch," he says, placing the glass on the glossy cement floor. He narrows his eyes, and in an instant, a loud crack fills the room as the glass shatters into dust.

Finn sits back down, his gaze fixed on me, clearly waiting to see my reaction. I'm perplexed, my skepticism weakening as I start to believe him.

"You say you're a vampire," I begin, voice steadier than I feel. "Does that mean you drink people's blood?"

"Only if granted permission," he replies calmly.

I'm confused. That's not how it works in vampire stories. "If they *let* you?"

"It's not like the movies. Every creature has limits," he says, his voice quieter as he adds, almost to himself, "Except humans."

"So you never drink blood? Who would actually let you do that?"

He lets out a scoffing snort. "You'd be surprised."

My heart skips a beat. There's a question hanging in the air, something deeply personal. I'm not sure I have the right to ask, but I can't stop myself. "When was the last time you drank a human's blood?"

"A long time ago."

The response is clipped, and I can tell he doesn't want to talk about it, but I push forward, my curiosity too strong. "What happens if no one gives you their blood? Do you die?"

He looks uncomfortable, and I realize I'm treading on thin ice, but I need to know. "We call it being parched. It doesn't kill you, but it makes you *want* to die."

"Are you parched?" The words slip out before I can stop them.

"No. I haven't been parched since I moved here."

"To Cleveland?"

"No, here." He sweeps the dim room with his intense gaze. "This apartment. I presume it's because I'm near *you*."

I flinch, taken aback. "So you think I'm the reason you're not 'parched'?"

"Yes. I didn't know why until tonight. I've been watching you."

"Watching me?" I'm shocked again.

"Your name is Glo Slater. You're from Cerritos, California. There isn't one picture of you on file anywhere, not even at the DMV. Did you know that?"

"That's crazy." I fish my driver's license out of my wallet and flash it at him. "See? Right here."

"That's not the Glo Slater who lives at your address, according to the DMV. You also have two parents. Cause of death: plane crash."

"What? No! They were killed in a car accident!" I practically shout. "This is insane."

"Revolution Ways Airline, Flight 5403, from Rochester, New York, to Auckland, New Zealand."

"They were hit by a truck while driving from Cincinnati to Toledo," I say, my voice rising with frustration.

"There isn't a single photo of your parents on file anywhere. In reality, you and your parents don't exist."

I throw up my hands. "Wait!" The information is coming at me so fast, I can hardly process it.

I shut my eyes, taking a deep breath, holding it in before releasing it slowly. Maybe this isn't real. Maybe it's part dream, part nightmare.

"Do you believe me now?" His voice is steady, waiting.

Despite the madness of it all, the answer comes

quickly, with a certainty that surprises me. Eyes still closed, I whisper, "I do."

"Open your eyes," he whispers. His voice is gentle, like a soft spring breeze, and before I know it, my eyes flutter open.

"I noticed you're a hider," he says. "You shouldn't hide from this. I need you."

His words catch me off guard, striking deep. I swallow hard, surprised he's figured me out so quickly. "You need me? For what?"

"I'm a slayer," he reveals, his tone calm but intense.

I blink, my confusion growing. "What do you slay?"

"Vampires."

"But you're a vampire," I point out, my voice barely above a whisper.

"Yes, I am."

"You slay your own kind?" The question feels heavy, like I'm stepping into a world I wasn't prepared for.

"Yes, I do," he answers, without a trace of hesitation.

"So you're like Van Helsing?" I joke, trying to lighten the weight of the moment. I've never been good with heavy atmospheres.

Finn chuckles, though it's faint. "Van Helsing isn't real. I am."

But something doesn't sit right with me. The way he's looking at me. It feels like there's an expectation. I shake my head, trying to clear the thought. "I'm not killing vampires."

He tilts his head slightly, his gaze piercing. "Do you have a choice?"

I've had enough. I spring to my feet, and he stands too, the sudden closeness between us making the air feel heavy. We haven't been this near since we first collided.

"You'll have to join me," he says, his tone firm. "Sooner rather than later."

"Is that supposed to be a riddle?" My voice comes out sharper than intended, but I can't help it.

"No, it's not a riddle," he replies. "One day, someone you know will be attacked by a vampire. The lines that once clearly separated our worlds have started to blur."

"The line between vampires and humans?"

"Yes. But not my kind—a different kind."

I take a second to absorb what he's saying. "There are different kinds of vampires?"

"Yes."

"And these other vampires… they're the ones attacking humans?"

He moves closer, so close that the tips of our noses nearly touch. "I'm telling you they already have."

A cold shiver runs down my spine. Before I can respond, there's a knock on my door across the hall.

"Glo," Aries calls, her voice unmistakable. "Are you home?"

Finn's words hang in the air, but my attention shifts to the familiar sound of my best friend calling from just feet away.

"Why don't you give it some more thought?" he suggests just as the knock sounds again, a little louder this time.

I swallow hard, caught between two worlds.

We both watch in silence as Aries moves through my apartment, peeking into each room. She calls my name softly, almost as if she knows I'm close but just out of reach.

"How in the world?" I whisper, utterly floored by the fact that she just unlocked my door without a key.

"Your friend isn't human either," Finn says, his voice low.

I whip my head around to him. "What is she, then?"

He shakes his head, his brow furrowed. "I don't know."

My heart is racing now. "Does she want to hurt me?"

He narrows his eyes, studying her closely. "I don't think so. She seems more like a protector. Whatever makes me—"

"Shush!" I whisper sharply, cutting him off as Aries moves back toward the front door. She hesitates, standing in the hallway, then glances down the corridor before stopping in front of Finn's door.

I freeze, holding my breath, watching her as she looks up and down the hall. After what feels like an eternity, she finally turns toward the elevator. But before she steps in, she glances back toward Finn's door, her gaze lingering. Then, just as quickly as she came, she's gone, slipping into the passenger seat of a sleek red sports car where Raz waits behind the wheel.

"I can't hear her," I whisper frantically, my voice shaky with frustration.

Finn's voice is calm, almost reassuring. "Let yourself hear her, and you will."

Desperate to know what she's saying to Raz, I

do as Finn suggests. The moment I focus, the world around me sharpens, and I gasp as Aries' voice suddenly becomes clear.

"She's not in her apartment, but I know she's around," Aries says, her tone certain.

I'm not sure if I should feel relieved or even more terrified.

"Maybe she has a boyfriend in the building."

"No." Aries scowls up at my window. "She would've told me."

"She doesn't tell you everything, babe."

After a minute, she says, "Maybe not. But remember, I can read her mind."

I gasp again.

"Yeah," Raz says.

"What the hell," I growl.

"Something's blocking me, though. It's deliberate," Aries says.

"Can't she block you?"

"If she knows too, but I don't think she does."

I'm glad to hear that. From this day forward, she's *blocked*.

"Just call her in the morning, and I'll keep an eye out too," Raz says.

Aries nods. That's when the car speeds away from the curb.

I lose all the feeling in my legs and flop back down into the chair. I am overwhelmed, as if the Niagara Falls is crashing down on me. She can read my mind? She can go into my locked apartment without a key? Seriously?

Finn remains quiet with me.

He digs a folded piece of paper out of his pants pocket and holds it out to me. "Can I ask you to do me a favor?"

I look at the square of paper for a moment. "What?" I snap because I'm still angry.

"In the morning, go here and then tell me what you see and hear," he says, unaffected by my tone.

I take the paper and unfold it. There's an address and a time on it. "What's this?"

"You'll see. Just watch, and come see me tomorrow when the sun goes down. I'll be waiting."

Since I really need to be alone, I nod and leave. Aries had the wherewithal to lock the door behind her—talk about deceptive. A twenty-eight-year friendship built on lies? Although I'm furious, I'm not surprised.

I'm not crazy. There is a bubble. My God, *there is a bubble*.

CHAPTER 3
ZOMBIES

I lie in bed staring at the ceiling for half the night. Then I watch a movie star, whose name eludes me, peddling the Sluggers Workout program on Paid Programming TV for the other half. Basically, I get absolutely no sleep. I can't stop thinking about everything that happened during the wee hours of the morning.

My neighbor's name is Finn, and he says he's a vampire, which I eighty percent believe. My best friend can read my mind, and I wonder why. Even Raz knows she can. What does he mean by "he'll check in on me later"? Does he plan to stop by? This is all insanity. However, it's no crazier than being able to see through barriers, burn things with your eyes, or shatter a glass into dust with them. And really, this guy Finn is a vampire slayer?

I lean over to retrieve the folded piece of paper Finn gave me from the coffee table. *11:00 a.m.* That's the time Finn wants me to be at the address off 40th Street. I don't have to go into work today, which means I have all morning to ponder whether I should do this or not.

I wonder what Finn's doing. Does he sleep in a crypt during the day? Dracula sleeps in one. At least, that's the legend. As I slip out of my green fluffy robe, standing in nothing but my underwear, I wonder if he's ever seen me this way, and if so, how many times? The possibility of him watching me makes me self-conscious about taking a shower. Although it wouldn't be wise to forgo taking one only because my neighbor might cheat and see me naked.

So I strip out of my panties and bra, hop into the warm shower, and wash up as fast as I can. A few minutes later, I dry off, slip into a heavy pair of jeans, fur-lined, knee-high snow-boots, and a button-down green, yellow, and black plaid shirt. My hair has grown back down to my lower back, so I fish a pair of scissors out of the top drawer of the cabinet in the bathroom and cut my hair shoulder length.

"There," I whisper after examining myself in the mirror. I look fresh without so much hair. It's a good look.

As I play with the idea of visiting the address Finn gave me, I slip into my black tweed coat. It's thick and has proven to keep me warm when the temperature dips way low. Once I turn the doorknob to leave, my cell phone, which is sitting on the coffee table, rings. After a brief hesitation, I choose not to answer it. I don't have to be clairvoyant to know who's calling.

The diner downstairs is pretty crowded. We're one of the only places open on New Year's. Dora, Lucy, and Samantha are working, and Manny is behind the register, counting cash. He owns the place, so the more bills that end up in the slots, the better his mood. On a slow day, he's the crabbiest person in the world. He's even worse on payday. He really hates to give the cash away.

Once I offered to let him keep my check. He'd just asked me what the hell I was talking about and shoved the check back at me. I was afraid to tell him that I didn't need the money; I could work for free. He might find that insulting or decide to fire me and give my job to someone whom he thinks needs it. *I need it.*

"Glo!" Sam sings my name as soon as she sees me.

Sam is, by all accounts, beautiful. Her skin is the color of cream, and her blond hair is natural. She pairs her fair characteristics with bold red lipstick. To the chagrin of almost all of our male customers, she's happily married with two children. She's only twenty-five. That combination is rare in California. The age at which people settle down in Cleveland was something I needed to adjust to when I moved here seven years ago. I love a sea of good-looking single guys, preferably those who have never been divorced and are above college age. This city is not a single lady's paradise.

Sam puts her hand at the corner of her mouth and whispers, "Hey, somebody's been waiting for you. He's hot."

I'm halfway expecting to see Finn, but when I look across the floor, Upton is sitting alone at a table for two, grinning at me.

"Hey, did you just call my cell?" I ask her.

"Yeah, but I guess you were on your way here." Sam flutters her eyebrows at Upton. "He's so hot.

Man, he's hot. He even has an accent. Did you know he has an accent?"

She's talking very fast, but I'm only barely concentrating on what she's saying. I was one-hundred-percent sure Aries had been the one calling. It's not like her to give up so easily, especially when she's trying to track me down.

"Yeah, I know, he's pretty cute," I say.

"No, he's hot," she corrects me.

"Okay, hot," I say with a sigh. I walk over and take the seat across from Upton.

The first thing he does is study my face. "Very well. Last night wasn't a dream."

"That's what I said this morning," I say with a smile as I wiggle out of my coat and hang it on the back of my chair. "So how did you know I'd be here?"

"Aries told me you have breakfast here every morning." He twists his neck to study the diner. "What is this anyway? It's not a café, is it? Doesn't smell like one."

"Good question." I grin at him. "Diner food, café looks."

"Ah, nice combination. Greasy yet crumbly," he says with a wink. "So you left before the ball ended."

I chuckle, finding the Cinderella reference quite charming. "Yeah." I sigh. "Sorry about that. I had to leave."

"Whatever for?"

I hesitate as a picture of Finn forms in my mind. Even that mental image of him causes my heart to thump. The embarrassing part is that I don't think he's attracted to me romantically. He only wants me to be the Robin to his Batman. I would be a fool to not stay in *this* moment with *this* guy.

Upton is extremely attractive. His eyes, nose, and mouth remind me of that Scottish actor, Gerard Butler. Just looking at him makes me wish Finn had never showed up last night. Who knows how things would've progressed between the two of us. I could've awakened this morning with a new boyfriend, which wouldn't have been so bad. It's about time for that.

"I know it was rude of me to leave after saying I was going to the loo, and I apologize," I say, leaving out all the bizarre details.

"You did say loo, didn't you?"

I blurt a chuckle. "I did."

"Speaking English now, are you?"

"Unfortunately, I start and stop at loo. I mean, I

can throw in a few bloodies and brilliants, but only if the opportunity arises."

"Good then, how about dinner tonight?"

"Tonight?" I hesitate because, again, thoughts of Finn get in the way of my answer. "Okay. Deal."

"All right then." He looks around the busy diner. Almost every table is taken. "You live here?"

"I do. Upstairs, unit 810."

"All right then. What time should I pick you up?"

A picture of Finn threatens to pop up in my head, but I erase it before it forms. "How about eight? Is that too late?"

"Not at all," he says and slips on his coat, preparing to leave.

"You're not having breakfast?"

"Definitely *not*. Wouldn't want a diner"—he sort of turns up his nose—"to be where we have our first date. Would you?"

I shrug. "It doesn't matter to me."

"It will once I show you how impressive I am." He smirks, sure of himself. "Sound a bit smarmy, don't I?"

"Ah, another Briticism," I purr.

He lets out a light laugh. "Tell you what; I'll show you what smarmy means tonight at dinner.

That way you won't think I'm an ass." He winks while wearing that sexy grin of his, one side of his top lip raised high.

I think I'm grinning too. He's charmed my socks off, and I must admit, he has me where he wants me. I can hardly wait until eight o'clock.

AFTER UPTON LEAVES, I ORDER PANCAKES TOPPED with fresh blueberries. As I sip on a cup of coffee and wait for my order to arrive, Aries walks in. My heart sinks. I have no idea what to say to her. I thought I wanted to let her have it for lying to me for so many years, but after seeing her face, I'm less incensed and more hurt. All I want to do is beg her to explain herself, but the place is pretty crowded. A conversation like the one we should have isn't intended for others to hear. They'd think we were two crazy ladies who should be committed. I can just picture it.

"I know you can read my mind," I'd say.

She would deny it, of course.

"I saw and heard you in the car with Raz."

I'd want her to say, "You weren't in the car with us?"

Then I could say, "No, that's because I was in a neighbor's apartment. His name is Finn, and he's a vampire. We both could look right through the walls and see you—oh, and hear you—in the car with Raz! Now explain yourself, please."

Goodness, what a disaster it would be to have *that* conversation in public.

As she sits down in Upton's empty seat, she starts off by saying, "Hi." She has the audacity to sound huffy!

Clearly, she has no clue that I know what I know. She's playing the guilt game that's worked so many times before. The difference is now I *know* I have nothing to feel guilty about.

"Hi," I reply just as huffily.

"What happened to you last night?"

"I left."

"I know that. You didn't say good-bye."

"Didn't know I had to."

The four guys at the table next to us are following our tension-filled exchange. We sound as if, at any second, we might escalate to ripping out each other's hair.

"It's just, I don't know…" Aries shrugs one shoulder, feigning nonchalance. With forced calm, she says, "Rude."

"Really?" I feign shock and lean across the table toward her. "How about entering someone's apartment without a key? Is that rude?"

I fall back in my chair. One of the guys has been hanging on my every word, and he glances at Aries. By the way he's sitting, I can tell he's listening for a response.

But she doesn't say anything. She just stares at me like a kid caught with her hand in the cookie jar. I think I know what she's trying to do—read my mind. So I let her. I show her how I saw her unlock my door without a key. I show her that I heard and saw her conversation with Raz. And that's it. I show her nothing about Finn.

Aries turns to the guy at the other table, who's shamelessly watching her now. After a moment, he turns to one of his friends and announces he's ready to go. One by one, they all clear out.

I lean across the table and whisper, "What did you just do to them?" I'm not happy about the Jedi mind tricks she's playing on those unsuspecting people.

"We need to talk," she whispers.

"What are you going to do? Clear out the whole diner?"

"I see that you don't want me to do that," she says, which is a strange reply.

"I didn't want you to make those guys leave either."

That's when the craziest thing happens. They come back inside, take their seats and resume eating like nothing happened.

I gasp. "Twenty-eight years," I say through clenched teeth. "Twenty-eight years."

"Let's go upstairs," she suggests.

I shake my head. "I have to eat, and then I have an errand to run and a date tonight, thanks to you."

"Upton?"

"Tell me, is he anything like you?"

After a moment, Aries shakes her head. "He's not what I am."

I'm so hurt. I think she's broken my heart. I've always had my suspicions, but I hoped the truth would be different. I wanted my best friend, who's more like my sister, to be a normal, everyday woman. I wanted to be the crazy one for suspecting anything different.

"You saw me?" she asks. Her face is marked with concern.

"Didn't know that I knew to look, did you?"

"I didn't," she confesses.

Does she look sad? I'm looking into her eyes, and I can't tell. There's something in them though.

"How about tomorrow morning?" I say. "Let's talk then."

"You just have a date with Upton tonight? That's all?"

I frown suspiciously. "Why?"

Before she can answer, Sam walks over and sets my breakfast in front of me. "Good morning, Aries." She sings her name the way she sang mine. "Can I get you something?"

Aries, who's normally equally friendly to everyone who crosses her path, glances up with a forced half-smile. "Good morning, Sam. No, thank you." There's not even an ounce of warmth in her tone.

Sam lifts her eyebrows, signaling that she felt the chill.

"Tomorrow morning then," Aries says to me before standing. She looks down, waiting for my reply.

"All right," I barely say.

We give each other one last look before she whips around and strides out the door. Through the window, Sam and I watch her climb into Raz's red sports car and speed off down the icy road.

"What's wrong with her?" Sam asks.

I shrug and whisper, "I don't know."

"Humph" is all the thought Sam gives it before sitting in the empty chair across from me. "Okay, it's break time. Tell me about the guy from this morning. He's so hot. How did you meet him?"

I eat and tell her about Upton until ten thirty a.m. The walk is about forty-five minutes, so after leaving a tip and saying good-bye to Sam and the other waitresses, I head out to the address Finn gave me.

IT'S A HOLIDAY BUT A MAJOR SHOPPING DAY AT THE same time. People are out spending money, even in the snow. I decide to walk the back roads that run parallel to Payne Avenue because sometimes I walk so fast it scares people. As I hoof it under the freeway overpass, the astringent odor of urine makes me want to puke. As I leave the city, I walk across train tracks, past an empty lot and a church. There's hardly any traffic at all since there's hardly anywhere to shop over here.

I unfold the paper again to check the address. I'm pacing in front of an empty lot, but I'm pretty sure this is the right place. Since Finn was so adamant that I come here, I decide that I won't just leave and report that I saw nothing. Apparently, there *must* be something to see.

I pivot, using only my primary vision to search in all directions as I turn. I see nothing out of the ordinary. Some guy gets into a white weather-stained pick-up truck and drives off. He doesn't look suspicious. The longer I stand here, the colder I get. I know that I have to use my secondary vision in order to give Finn a full report, so this time, I let myself see through the old buildings surrounding me. A lot of them are abandoned shop floors, but they're not located at the address Finn wrote down —the vacant field is.

That's when I set my eyes back on the vacant lot. I notice cement lines trace it, as if at one time, a building used to be here. It's a long shot, but my instincts tell me to see what's going on underground.

Bingo.

If my eyes aren't deceiving me, then there's a full-on chemical lab beneath the surface. It's not empty either. Two people are in it, mixing up solutions while wearing biohazard suits. I let myself hear what's going on down there. They're not talking, but a minute later, I hear a buzz. The two people in suits nod at each other. I watch them walk out of the main lab area and into a small empty chamber. They pull off their head gear. They're both men.

They're soon joined by a man wearing designer blue jeans—I can tell by the way the pockets are designed—and a gray blazer. He's also wearing Italian-cut loafers, which is way out of season being it's almost twenty degrees outside.

The guy with the loafers says, "How many do we have in this shipment?"

"Fifty," one of the men replies.

"That's all?" He sounds disappointed. "What the hell have you been doing here all week?"

"It takes four hours to make one Zombie, and we can only process three at a time. We told you this. Didn't we?"

The two men, who I assume are chemists, glance at each other. They're tense, as if they're afraid of this guy.

"Do I look like I give a damn about what you said?" he growls.

One of the chemists says, "Well—"

As soon as he opens his mouth, the guy in the fancy jeans gets right in his face before I can finish blinking. As I gasp, the chemist gulps; his eyes are as wide as a guppy's.

"We can double, maybe triple the number if you get us more equipment," chemist number two chimes in. He hesitates before he adds, "And a little help."

Then once again, my eyes deceive me. In the next second, the guy in the loafers has the man who asked for help pinned against the wall by the collar of his biohazard suit.

"There. Is. No. Help," Loafer Guy declares through his clenched teeth. He lets the chemist crash against the cement floor. "It behooves you to remember that although I can't kill you, I can make you wish you were dead," Loafer Guy continues. He snatches the bag of white pills, which I think are called Zombies, from the chemist he didn't choke. "Next time I want three hundred. You have two days."

The chemists watch him leave with sheer terror in their eyes. I decide to let my eyes follow the guy in the loafers through an unlit tunnel that extends way past our city. He's moving so fast that I lose sight of him. When I see that Loafer Guy is good and gone, I put my focus back on the chemists.

"As long as the sun's out, we're safe," one of them says.

"The sun's out now," the other shouts, shaking a hand toward the sky. "And remember that fog. Three fucking hundred! We won't be able to get that many done in two days, and he knows it. It's an excuse. He wants to kill us. We got to get the hell out of here!"

"And go where?"

"Siberia, damn it. Anywhere but dead."

"Let's just try."

"It can't be done."

"Maybe we can cut a little bit. I think they're too strong anyway," one says.

"Talk to me."

"It takes the R-trampine-V four hours to process. If we remove it, we can cut a thousand Zombies a day."

The other chemist is silent for a moment. "You ever wonder?"

"Wonder what?"

"What they're doing with this shit?"

"They don't pay us to care," the other chemist says.

"It's just... Forget it." The guy sighs. "Vez-B. Let's try that as a substitute."

The two men don their biohazard head-coverings and head back into the lab.

I don't know what to think about this. A guy who moves faster than I ever thought possible is making chemists cut drugs called Zombies for him. That's the report.

IT'S ONLY ONE IN THE AFTERNOON WHEN I GET home, and the sun doesn't go down until around five o'clock this time of year. I pace across my living room as I wait. I can't help but remember how fast the man in the fancy loafers moved. Something tells me he's a vampire and prey to a vampire slayer like Finn.

I can't believe I made a date with Upton tonight of all nights. The deep knot in my stomach put there by that chemist who was scared out of his mind won't go away. I need to help him. I feel as though I can somehow. I can't wait to tell Finn that in this case, I'll help him slay *a* vampire if that's what it takes to free them.

My doorbell rings.

I'm getting used to seeing with my second sight, so I look right through the door to see who it is. It's

Aries. I knew she wouldn't be able to wait until tomorrow morning. Patience has never been a virtue of hers. Yes, she lied to me, but that doesn't change how I feel about her. She's still my friend, and I still love her.

I take a deep breath to clear my thoughts and yell, "Come in." I know she doesn't need me to unlock the door for her.

When she steps inside, I can't help but notice that she's wearing a sexy red-and-white chain-link patterned wrap dress with a pair of ultra-high stilet-tos. She's not wearing a coat or even a jacket. She dresses like this all the time during the winter, but I always figured it stemmed from vanity. I love her, but she can be vain. She's not the sort of vain that dumps on other people. She just loves beauty in everything: other human beings, animals, clothes, cars, places, and even herself. Right now, I'm wondering if there's another reason why she dresses so light in the freezing cold.

"What are you, Aries?" I ask after she sits in the red chair. I sit across from her on the sofa. I halfway expect her to dance around my question.

"I'm one of your guardians. Charles and Rachel were your primary guardians."

My mouth falls open. I can't believe she told the

truth right out. After recovering from shock, I ask, "Why do I need a guardian?"

She narrows her eyes and stares into mine. "Remember when I worked as a nanny for about seven years?"

"Vaguely," I say.

"I worked with a girl named Clarity. She's your sister."

I blink a number of times—maybe I'll wake up. "Did you just say I have a sister?"

Aries closes her eyes and sighs. "I'm not supposed to tell you any of this, but…"

She keeps her eyes closed. The heaviness in the room overwhelms me. I've never seen her this way. I'm almost panicked—not because of what she just revealed but because of her state of being. However, I hold firm. I need her to tell me everything.

"So Rachel and Charles had another daughter?" I ask, sounding resilient.

It's actually sort of refreshing to learn my parents had skeletons in their closet. Their perfection made them creepy.

Aries opens her eyes. "Didn't you hear me? I said they were your guardians, not your parents."

"Then who are my parents?"

Again, she hesitates. "If I tell you, then you can't see me again after today. Are you ready for that?" That's when tears fall from her eyes, and she wipes them. I go over to give her a hug, and she chuckles in pure delight. "I didn't know I could do that!"

I laugh with her. "I didn't know you could either!"

Aries takes my hands, and we sit side by side on the sofa.

"Let me tell you about myself first," she says. "Then you can decide if you want me to continue. I've been alive for four thousand human years. I was made to guard the Life Blood."

"Four thousand years?" I marvel. "Are you screwing with me?" I've never known her to joke around like that.

"No, I'm not." She looks and sounds earnest.

Then I feel and say the oddest thing. "I believe you." I really do believe her. "And I don't want you to go anywhere. So don't tell me anything else."

We sit in silence. The tension is thick between us as the seconds tick by. I think it's because we both know that even though she didn't tell me the rest, I still know too much. Vampires exist. My parents weren't my parents. My friend is four thousand years old. She can read my mind and control the minds of others. We no longer have a choice. She has to tell me.

So she closes her eyes and sighs. "You're the last of the hidden Life Blood."

I have no idea what that means, but I'm sure it has something to do with my eyes.

"You have what humans call a grandmother. She lived in 5000 BC. She was from a village in what is now the northern part of Africa. Her name was Zillael. One of your sisters shares her name."

"What do you mean *one* of my sisters?"

"Let me finish." She squeezes my hand as if she fears that at any moment, she'll disappear into thin air. "Zillael, your grandmother, was the last *mu-se-el*. It's a celestial term for a direct communicator with the Creator. Back then, people were turning to idols. Wood statues with names that I will not repeat," she says through gritted teeth. "A bad spirit had grown stronger. It called itself *the evil*. The humans who worshipped *the evil* started drinking blood. The more they drank, the less human they became.

"Zillael came to what is now called the Blue Nile to pray for the people. She asked for forgiveness for them. But it was too late. *The evil* was prevailing, mastering its power. That's why Zillael was impregnated by a being you call angels and taken to a universe called Enu."

She stops and studies my expression. I know she's waiting for me to react, but I have no reaction. Of course all of this could sound insane, and to anyone else, it would. But not me. With every word she says, I feel myself lifting higher and higher on my way up to smash right through the bubble.

"I'm fine. Go on," I assure her.

"She had a son, your father. Felix of the House of Benel, which is the house of her human father. She died in Enu because without the love of the baby inside her, she couldn't live. It takes five seconds for a human to die in Enu. That's not long enough for a baby to see and fall in love with his mother."

"That's heartbreaking," I whisper.

"Yes, it was."

"If the baby had known to love her, then she could've lived in this place you're talking about?"

"Her heart was pure, so yes, she could've," Aries says.

"Who took care of her child?"

"His name as Meni'he. The English translation is Mountain."

"A man took care of him?"

"Meni'he is not a man. He's a male Enuian. Male and female Enuians are equally nurturing."

"Oh." I must admit, I love the thought of that.

"Here's how you came to be, Gu'he."

My throat is tight, but I manage to mutter, "Glo. Gu'he is Glo."

"Yes, that's your Enuian name. You're not all human."

I think back to when Finn said I didn't smell human and neither did Aries. Dear goodness. Everything he said is true!

"What am I then?" I ask.

"Felix fell in love with Ce'lah'ime—"

"Crystalline?" I ask. But as a matter of fact, I *know* that's what Ce'lah'ime means.

"Yes, that's the English translation. Felix and Ce'lah'ime had seven daughters: you and your six sisters. All of you were born to thwart the ambitions of *the evil*."

I'm still speechless, but I do have a question. "These people who drink blood sound like vampires. Am I supposed to fight vampires?"

"I know about Finn," she confesses.

I flinch, taken aback. "You do?"

"Yes, and I don't understand, but you're not the

only sister bonded to a vampire. I don't know why, but he's not the enemy."

"Okay," I whisper. Another question pops in my head. "What about this sister of mine? Why didn't you ever tell me about her?"

"I couldn't. You were hidden, and she was hidden. Now neither of you are."

"I'm not?"

"The day Finn found you, you were found," Aries says.

"Okay, but what does being found entail?"

"You'll see. Vampires can smell you now. They'll know you have the Life Blood. Here's what you need to know though. A vampire can't drink your blood without your permission, but watch out. A Sham has already tried to make a human kill Clarity. They could try to come after you too. It didn't work, and Egos was able to kill the Shams who'd conjured the magic."

"Who's Egos?"

"Viesel Egos is Cl'auta's Guardian who wields the sword. He's only able to fight and protect. You'll meet Echo Leon when the time comes. He's your Guardian who wields the sword."

"I see," I say. Needing an Echo Leon is the first

scary thing she's said to me. "And these Shams...
What are they, witches?"

"They're conjurers and spell spinners. They're
no good." Aries shakes her head as if she's trying to
get the thought of Shams out of it.

"I see." I stand and gaze down at her. She looks
up at me with the saddest eyes. "Do you want a
drink? I have a good burgundy in the kitchen."

Aries smiles. "I didn't expect you. You know
that?"

"What do you mean?"

"You're my friend. My sister. In the human way.
It was unexpected."

I look toward the kitchen. I'm almost afraid to
leave the room because it sounds as though she's
saying good-bye. I don't want to come back to find
her gone, so I sit back down on the edge of the sofa.
"What's next?"

She shakes her head. "Honestly, I don't know. I
thought that after I told you, I'd be over."

"Do you mean dead?"

"No, not dead. I thought I'd simply no longer
exist."

I squeeze her hand. "I don't want you to no
longer exist."

"Relax, Glo." She squeezes my hand to calm

me down. "It's not in you or me to fear these things. Is it?"

I ponder how I truly feel about her being erased, and I sigh. "I just don't want to lose you."

Her eyes gaze upward, as if they can see the sky through the ceiling and the two flats above mine. "I'm still here."

"But for how long?"

She shakes her head. "I don't know."

"Okay," I barely say, trying to convince myself to be okay with the possibility of losing her. "So are you still my Guardian?"

"Always. As long as I'm on Earth, I'm a Guardian to the Daughters of the House of Benel."

"The what of what?" I ask with a chuckle, lightening the mood without trying to.

Aries laughs too, signaling the end of our heavy conversation. I go pour each of us a glass of wine, and I'm glad to find her sitting on the sofa when I return. She's even taken off her shoes and turned on the TV. She's watching a re-run of one of those reality shows she loves.

"You know she's come out with her own clothing line, and it's fab," Aries says about the stylist on the show.

I can hardly believe celestial guardians like Aries

exist. Ones who call clothes "fab" and love a good party on the French Riviera. Maybe what or who she is explains why everyone always has such a good time at her bashes. Her parties are a transcendental experience. I tell her about Finn and what I saw earlier today in the underground lab.

"I can't tell you what to do in this matter. What do you think you should do?" she asks me.

"I don't know," I say with a sigh.

"You'll figure it out. Are you still going out with Upton tonight?"

"Upton!" I almost forgot we have a date tonight.

"He's really into you, and he's one of the good ones. Remember that?"

Strange enough, I get it. "He's cute." I flop back against the sofa, feeling fully relaxed by the pricey burgundy. "He's charming too. He's really sexy…"

I'm waiting for her to chime in with a "but" like she normally does, but she remains silent while smiling.

"Come on, where's your unwanted advice?" I ask, grinning expectantly at her.

"He's human; you're not. Have you looked in the mirror, Glo? Not a lot of aging going on, is there?"

I recall all the contours of my face. My skin looks and feels like it did when I was seventeen years old. Back then, I looked older than everyone else my age. I'm forty-three! She's right; I shouldn't look like this.

"I don't want to marry him," I say. I just want to indulge in him.

"He likes you. You're beautiful and nice, and something about you makes him want to know you forever."

"How do you know this? Can you read his mind too?"

"The moment he became invested in you, I could," she says. "That's how I saw Finn in his head last night."

"Wow" is all I can say.

I think about her obscure warning even after we finish watching the reality show and she leaves. I forgot to ask her about Raz. What the heck is he? He's definitely something.

Before she left, we agreed to meet tomorrow for coffee, when I would let her know what happens between Upton and me tonight. It was my suggestion, of course. Something tells me Aries will see it all happening in real time.

CHAPTER 4
DECISIONS, DECISIONS

I stand at the window to watch the sun go down. Once it does, I brace myself before heading over to Finn's apartment.

One of our neighbors sees me knocking on his door. She's wearing a navy blue skirt suit; she must be returning home from work. I try not to meet her gaze, but I see her give me a very suspicious look. Apparently I'm not the only one who's noticed the sexy vampire who lives across the hall from me.

When I drop my face, I see how my appearance may stir her curiosity. I'm wearing a red, hooded, zip-up lounge dress and pair of white furry house-boots. I can imagine how scandalous my outfit looks. She could conclude that I'm sneaking across the hall for a night of sexual contact. If I hadn't already knocked, I would head back into my apartment and change into a baggy sweat suit.

I hear the girl's door open but not close. I peek in her direction and see her standing on the threshold, pretending to read mail, and making me antsy in the process. Finn hasn't answered yet, so I turn to head back to my apartment, admittedly relieved. That's when his door creeps open.

I peer through the crack; all I see is darkness. This could be his way of inviting me inside. So without giving the nosy person at the end of the hallway another chance to glance my way, I step inside and close the door. It's so dark in here that I can't see my hand in front of my face.

"Finn?" I stand very still because I feel a presence near me.

"I'm here," he says. That's when the dim lights switch on.

I sigh with relief. "Why didn't you just have the lights on when I walked in?" I'm holding my chest because my heart is pounding. I'm upset that he put me on display for the nosy neighbor and made me enter what feels like the torture room in a haunted house.

"Did you go?" he asks, ignoring my frantic disposition and question.

"Yeah." My pulse is slowing, but I'm still irritated. "I did."

"What did you see?"

I blink rapidly because he hasn't stepped back yet. He's still too close for comfort.

"Can I sit down?" I ask.

That's when Finn steps back, giving me space to pass. After I sit, he takes the seat across from me.

"Do I frighten you?" he asks after I get settled.

I can tell by the severe crease between his eyebrows that he's very interested in my answer. "Yes," I say, keeping it honest.

"I don't want to frighten you. What do I have to do to make you feel safe?"

I shrug. "You can start by not making me walk into a dark apartment."

"Sorry about that. I see better in the dark than in light. I'm not used to being alone with creatures of the day."

I flinch, taken aback by his declaration. "Really? You're never alone with people?"

"I told you. I'm a slayer. I hunt. That's it."

He's beginning to make sense. He's not a man or a monster; he's a machine. "I see."

"What did you see?" he asks, changing the context of my last remark.

I decide to go with it. "I saw a lab. Two men—chemists, I presume—were making white tablets called Zombies. There was a vampire in charge. I'm with you on slaying him. I'm all in for that."

Finn lifts one side of his mouth into a lopsided grin. "I don't need your help to slay Cort. I could kill him right now if I wanted to."

"Then I'm confused."

"You heard them refer to the Zombies?"

"Yes."

"You know what they're doing with those Zombies?" he asks. I can tell the question is rhetorical, and he continues without giving me a chance to speak. "Those pills have already wiped out two small towns, and they're working on the third."

"What do you mean by 'wiped out two small towns'?"

"They changed the dynamics of the population. Those who used to be human are now vampires, and those who chose not to become vampires were killed."

I gasp. I cannot believe what I just heard. "I understand that I'm not human, and you're a vampire. I've lived my whole life practicing remaining calm so that I don't charbroil someone. Being able to do that isn't normal, so I understand that the bizarre exists. But whole towns wiped out? That can't be kept a secret. Wouldn't the government or police get involved?"

My words came out sort of frantically, but Finn remains the picture of calm. "I'm sure the human authorities would get involved if they knew."

"I wish humans could handle this problem, but they can't. Your friend today, she mentioned Shams to you."

"Of course you listened in," I say.

"I did."

"What about Shams?"

"They have their methods."

He has me on the edge of my seat. "What methods?"

"They've obstructed electrical lines. They're experts at mimicking humans. I've seen them put borders around a town so no one can leave or enter. And that's only scratching the surface. I've seen them do a lot of destructive shit."

A chill runs up my spine. All this supernatural stuff leads me to a new thought. "Um, do you watch me, you know, when I shower or get dressed?"

His eyes fall down my body and across my chest in particular. "Do you really want to know the answer to that?"

By the look in his eyes, I'm pretty sure I already know it. I'm curious to see if he'll admit it. "I do."

"Yes," he replies.

We stare into each other's eyes. I'm not embarrassed or upset, nor do I feel violated. I'm intrigued. For the first time since I laid eyes on him, I think that he may at one point have been attracted to me, and that possibility gives me some hope.

"Follow me," he says as he stands. The shift in his tone signals a change of subject.

I follow him to a spot on the floor where we face the far right wall. He stands behind me and puts his hands on my shoulders. As soon as he touches me, a burst of warmth explodes inside me, filling me from head to toe.

I catch my breath. "What's happening?"

He lifts his hands off my shoulders. "The hell if I know." He sounds alarmed too.

I'm too afraid to turn and look at him, but I want to. Heck, I want to do more than that. I want to fall through his skin and become one with him.

After a moment, he puts his hands back on me. This time, he touches the sides of my head. "Your hair grew back."

"Yeah," I say tentatively, surprised he noticed. Normally after I cut it to shoulder length, it takes three to four days to grow back down to my waist, but this time, it grew back in less than a day.

He gently positions my head where he wants it. The warmth returns. I want to shiver but force myself not to because that would be embarrassing.

"Look straight ahead," he whispers. "When you get to the empty lot, look downward."

I follow his instructions. I see through barriers, past the lives of others eating, laughing, walking, talking, driving, making love, kissing, holding hands, and watching TV. I get to the vacant lot and tilt my head downward.

"Are you there?" he whispers thickly.

I wonder if he's *trying* to seduce me. "Yes." I'm breathing heavily.

He turns my head a little to the left and then up. "Do you see that?"

I swallow hard. The warmth… I can hardly stand it. "I do."

There's a flat one-story building not too far from the empty lot. It's a shelter of some sort. It has a kitchen, dining hall, and rooms with rows of beds.

"Follow the stairs," he tells me.

There's a stairwell at the back of the building that leads to the basement. At the end of it is another gigantic sleeping quarters. Children and women lounge on the many beds. The room is an L-shape that loops around the lab.

"Wow," I whisper. "Those dirty bastards."

"They think I won't destroy it because of that," Finn whispers.

"You won't, will you?"

"I can," he answers.

"You'd kill those innocent people?"

"I haven't, have I?"

We fall silent between us. His hands slide down my shoulders to my ribcage to my waist. He lifts his hands off of me, leaving my entire body tingling.

"This is the start of a war, Glo," he says.

I wait for him to step back so that I can turn to face him. *Why won't he step back?* "I take it you need me for it?" I whisper, still affected by his nearness.

"When Cort comes back, we need to follow him. I can't do it without you. The Shams can't detect me as long as I'm near you."

"Because we're bonded or something? That's what Aries said."

"Yes, I heard that."

Fueled by a flash of ire, I whip around despite how close he is. "You listened to our entire conversation! Don't you sleep in a crypt during the day or something?"

"Yes, I did, and no, I don't." Of course he's completely composed and unaffected by my outburst.

I sigh hard, right in his face. He still doesn't budge. Instead, he leans in a little closer.

"So you watch me naked and listen to my conversations," I whisper. I meant to say that louder.

"*Watched* you naked," he corrects. "I apologize for that. You have a beautiful body. I couldn't always turn away, but I will now."

Oh goodness... He's left me lightheaded again. This time, I don't ask if I can sit; I just do it.

"Are you coming with me?" he asks as I slump into the hard chair. He's staring as if he's ignorant of the effect he has on me.

I pull it together enough to think about my job at the diner. Then Aries. Then Dr. Herman. I picture myself with jets under my boots. My hands are lifted high, and I'm blasting up toward the walls of the bubble. Then I remember.

"Oh God! I have a date!" I leap out of the chair.

In a blink of an eye, Finn is right in front of me. "I'm not pressuring you, Glo. If you decide not to accompany me, I'll find another way."

"No," I protest, shaking my head. "I'll do it. I just have a date. Do we have to leave now?"

He hesitates before shaking his head.

"Okay," I say. "You'll let me know when?"

He nods.

"Okay."

Silence falls between us. I want to get out of here as fast as I can, but I can't help watching him watch me. I look down to see what he finds so interesting. Goodness, my nipples are protruding against the material of my dress. I cross my arms. I've never wanted anyone more than I want him at this moment. I sigh in relief when Finn whips around, turning his back to me.

"I'll see you later," he says.

"All right," I reply to his backside.

Before I walk out the door, he says, "I think you should heed your friend's warning. Humans are fragile."

I know he's referring to Upton and our date tonight. "I'll remember that." I close the door behind me.

———

I HAVE AN HOUR TO PREPARE FOR UPTON'S ARRIVAL. I shower, trusting that Finn is keeping his eyes to himself. As I run my soapy hands across my abdomen, I can't help but recall what he said. He thinks my body is beautiful. He couldn't keep his eyes off my breasts. I look down at them. The funny thing about body parts is that that's all they are until a man admires them or, even better, touches them. Then, they become the conduits that usher in the gratification of being desired.

I'm hundreds of miles away from being a virgin. I've had my share of rolls in the hay, but not with just anyone. Upton is my type. He hasn't pulled out his wallet and counted a stack of hundred-dollar bills in front of me. He didn't invite me to his villa at some place with a name I'd forget as soon as it was spoken. His conversation was sort of awkward, as if he didn't know what to say to me, and it made him so endearing. In him lies the possibility of discovering a guy who won't repel me. I love engaging in the search for bliss.

As I step out of the shower and towel dry, I wonder if I should get to know Upton better or not. I've had experiences with British men before. I love them! Most of the time, British men come with no pretenses. They are who they are. I think it has a lot to do with being defined by their social hierarchies.

I've always loved observing human behavior. I studied social and cultural anthropology at Ohio State University. A duke is a duke is a duke, and a commoner is a commoner is a commoner. A man can buy a Ferrari or a Maserati or a villa in Cannes, but it doesn't change that he is who he is. Is his blood blue or red? I'm only into guys who are red-blooded and could never even begin to crave expensive cars and houses and titles or "striking" women. The look in Upton's eyes said he wants to *experience* me rather than *own* me. That's why I'm slipping on a black agora sweater dress and knee-high suede boots.

My date should be here in fifteen minutes. There's a possibility he might cancel though. The wind is banging against my large windows, and the sky is lobbing snow at them. Both are the recipe for a pretty remarkable snowstorm. As I stand at the window, gazing at the angry weather, I'm certain Upton will call at any moment. However, the doorbell chimes at five minutes before eight p.m., and I go answer it.

"Upton," I greet the cute guy standing across the threshold.

He's wearing a black beanie cap and a thick black wool coat. Both are soaking wet. "Bloody hell, it's shitty out there." He's clutching two full, wet paper bags contained in plastic bags. The bottle of wine clamped in his armpit is dripping water onto the floor.

I can't help but chuckle as I take the wine to alleviate the burden. "Well, you look beaten but not bruised!"

He's very attractive tonight, but his presence stirs a different feeling within me than Finn's does. I'm still not convinced that Finn won't disappear into thin air and never be seen again. He doesn't seem real. Upton is flesh and bone, and he doesn't have fangs.

"It's gone to shit out there. I had to leave the taxi on Woodland Avenue," he says.

"What were you doing way over on Woodland?" I ask. "I thought you were staying at the Hyatt?"

He lifts the bags. "Taste."

"The restaurant?"

"Aries said you're into fine dining."

"You went all the way over there in this weather? I'm impressed," I say.

"That was the point." Once he's fully inside my flat, he turns to examine the whole living room. "I don't think I've ever met anyone who lived so *slight*."

"Come on, I'll show you to the kitchen."

He's still twisting his neck, marveling at how understated I live. "However, it *is* quite nice… A lady bachelor's pad."

"Well, I *am* a bachelorette," I say with a chuckle.

We put the bags on the counter, and he studies my attire.

"You're all dressed up, and we have nowhere to go," he says.

I shrug. "I thought we were going out."

"I apologize on the weather's behalf," he says.

"I accept." I giggle as I take two plates and two wine glasses out of the cabinet.

Upton takes the containers of food out of the bags. "So I have sea scallops and blackened tilapia."

"Ah, Aries told you I like seafood."

"Should I say I instinctively knew what you like, or should I tell a fib?"

"Tell the fib." I chuckle, charmed by his humor.

"Well then, yes, I know your deepest desires."

We smile at each other until I offer to take his coat and cap. I hang them on a rack in my bedroom closet to dry off and look at the wall, wondering if Finn is watching us and listening to us. Something tells me he is.

Upton and I decide to eat in the living room on the floor in front of a toasty fire. The food is divine, as always.

After I ask what he does for a living, Upton says, "I'm a barrister."

"I never would've taken you for a lawyer."

"Well, I'm not *really*. I only deal with acquisitions and mergers."

"Ah. Business. That's how you're acquainted with my best friend."

He just grins.

"Are you acquainted with her in other ways?" I ask, wondering if that's what his silence means.

"We're mates, and Raz too, of course."

"Of course," I mutter. "What does he do? In all my years of knowing him, I've never bothered to ask."

"Never?"

"No."

"He's into sports. A professional surfer."

"Really?" I'm caught off guard by that. I knew he liked to surf—no, loved to surf—but I didn't think he did it for a living. "Has he ever won anything?"

"Absolutely! He's a champion. You really didn't know?"

"No, I didn't, but I'm not surprised. You couldn't keep him out of the ocean when we were growing up."

Again, he smiles. "Enough about him. What about you?"

I shrug and take a bite out of a scallop. "What do you want to know?"

"Do you enjoy being a waitress?"

Again, I shrug. I used to. Now, I don't know. After learning about myself, I feel as if my life has just begun.

"Yes? No? Maybe?" he says, urging me to answer.

"Probably not."

"Then why are you a waitress?" he asks.

"I like the people I meet."

"I bet you get hit on by a lot of blokes."

"Yeah, but what can I do about it?"

He chuckles. "You're very easy-going about it."

"That's because it takes two to make something happen. A guy can flirt, but I don't have to flirt back."

"Were you flirting with me last night?"

I flutter my eyelashes at him. "Indeed I was."

"I'm a lucky bastard then."

I can't help but chuckle. Goodness, he's so refreshing. I take a sip of wine, which has already put me at ease. "What do you want out of life, Upton?"

"At the moment, I desperately want you."

"How do you want me?" I stare into his eyes, eager to hear the right answer. When he breaks eye contact, I know my hopes have been dashed.

"Have you ever been to Prague?" he asks.

I sigh. The offer of doom. "Are you asking me to go to Prague with you?"

He waves a hand dismissively. "Only if you want. If you don't, then forget I ever mentioned it."

I know he's joking about the last part but not the first. *I don't want to go.*

"It's quite stunning this time of year, with the snow and the lights. We could stay at this old castle," he continues.

His offer hits me like a ton of bricks, over and over again. Aries warned me. After reading my mind all these years, she knows my wants, dislikes, fears, and everything. She cautioned me about this very moment.

I'm forced to say, "I'm not the kind of girl who enjoys being whisked away to Prague. Sorry."

"What kind of girl are you?"

Then I think. "Why didn't you bring burgers and fries?"

"You wanted a *hamburger*?" he says as if I'd just slapped him.

"No, I'm not saying I'd prefer a hamburger over scallops. But you asked me what I wanted."

"I think I'm confused." He stares at me, waiting for me to clarify.

I can't believe we're having this discussion. If he's upset now, he's going to really hit the ceiling after I spell out what I mean. Why couldn't he have just said that he wanted me flat on my back? This is a great night for passionate, no-strings-attached sex. After my encounter with Finn, I had been feeling sort of sexy. Now I feel like an object he wants to own. *Damn.*

"Forget it," I say. "Just no Prague. Sorry."

We eat in silence for quite a while. I hear a faint knock on a door. Not my door though—the one across the hall.

"Hello?" a female calls.

I whip my head around to look through the wall. The girl who lives down the hall is knocking on Finn's door. I let myself see inside his apartment. He's standing at the spot in the corner of the room, keeping his eyes on the lab; he's clearly ignoring her. Part of me wishes he was watching Upton and me. It would be nice to see him display a little jealousy. Nevertheless, one thing's for sure: Finn's not going to open the door for her. She checks over her shoulders, sees that the coast is clear, and turns the knob. It's locked. She whips around to stare daggers at my door before stomping back down the hallway. *What a psycho.*

When I face forward, I see Upton staring at me.

"Sorry," I say. "I thought someone was knocking on my door."

"So has this all gone to shit, or do I still have a chance in hell here?" he asks.

I look at him, but all I can think about is how Finn couldn't care less that I'm on a date with the "fragile human."

"I'm sorry?" I say, blinking myself back into the moment.

"Bloody hell, I've gone ahead and lost you."

"No, no, it's my fault. I just don't want to go to

Prague. I don't think I'm looking for anything serious. Are you?"

"Shit, no. I didn't say, 'Come on, Glo, let's tie the knot,'" he says.

"No—but don't you think Prague is a pretty big deal? I want Prague without realizing it's *Prague*." I shake my head, processing what I just said. "Heck, I don't even know what I just said means. I just know how it feels."

We turn silent again. I'm expecting him to announce that he should get going.

"Can I kiss you?" he asks.

I shrug. *Why not?* "Okay." I figure he's being polite. It's his one kiss before saying good-bye.

Upton leans toward me and puts his lips against mine. Oddly, he pauses as our lips touch. I'm confused and wondering if maybe he changed his mind until his warm tongue presses against my lower lip, waking up my mouth.

I've kissed many lips, and so far, he's the best kisser of them all. He lays me down on my back as his mouth explores mine. I forget being upset at Finn as Upton slips his hand under my dress and under my panties.

"Shit," he says. With that one touch, he knows I'm all into this.

Bam-bam-bam. The sound explodes in the room. We both stop. I'm sure his heart is beating as fast as mine—first from lust and now with panic.

Again, *bam-bam-bam.*

"Someone really wants in," Upton says breathlessly.

I'm still in a daze. I didn't expect Upton to have such good kissing skills. Heck, I'm almost ready to agree to go to Prague.

"I think they're gone," I whisper. "Maybe they had the wrong door."

"Oh," he says.

We get back to kissing. His hand is back under my dress, slipping one of my breasts out of my red satin bra. He's on his way to tasting his handiwork when—

Bam-bam-bam.

Glo! a man shouts in my head.

Now I know who it is. I didn't think he was paying attention. I sigh hard. "Just a moment." I scramble to fix my clothes.

"Should I come with you?" he asks, seeming reluctant to let me go.

"No need," I say. "I think I know who it is."

"Will you hurry back?" He's still holding my hand.

"I'll try," I say with a sigh. My legs are wobbly as I go over to answer the door.

Finn's eyes are wild, and his windblown hair is messier, as if he's been running his fingers through it. In a split second, the door to my apartment closes, and I'm inside his pitch-black apartment.

"What are you doing?" he growls.

I can't see his face. "What are *you* doing?"

My back is against the wall, and his body is pressed against mine. I'm stunned by the warmth that fills me.

"I need you to stop," he whispers. There's desperation in his voice.

"Stop what?" I snap. "I can't even move because you're pinning me against the wall."

"The human," he growls—actually *growls*. "Stop what you're doing with him."

"The kissing?"

"And everything else."

"But he's my date," I barely say.

"End it," he demands.

I swallow hard. I wish I could see his face. "Why?"

He doesn't say a word. I'm panting now. My body is more willing now than it was when Upton's lips, tongue, and hands seduced me. I *want* Finn to consume me the way Upton had. If Finn had asked me to go to Prague with him, I would've said yes—without hesitation, *yes*.

Finn's lips are near my ear. "End it. Please."

In another second, I'm back inside my apartment, facing the closed door.

"Where did you go?" Upton sounds a bit upset. "You were here, and then you disappeared."

"Sorry. My neighbor. He…" I stop to think of something to say.

"He?"

"Yeah, we're working on a project together." That's the truth.

"What sort of project?"

"We're watching over this homeless shelter. He was just giving me a report."

"I see." His expression shows that he's trying to figure out if he believes me.

I can't tell him that Finn's waiting for a vampire named Cort to return for the next shipment of Zombies so that we can follow him. After telling Upton that, he could probably have me legally committed.

However, Upton doesn't pursue his line of questioning. He pulls me back into him, and we're kissing again. But all I can hear is Finn's voice asking—rather begging—me to end my night with Upton.

"Where was I?" Upton's tongue trails up my neck as his hand smoothly lifts the hem of my dress. His fingers and tongue are like warm butter.

As I'm being forced to go against his will and push my dress back down, I whisper, "We were on the verge of doing things we shouldn't."

"Says who?"

I'm breathless as he nibbles on my bottom lip.

"You have a spectacular mouth," he whispers. "Is it yours?"

"Was I born with this mouth? Yes."

"Nice."

Now he's working on my top lip. I don't know what's happening to me. He's the first guy I've had sexual contact with in six months, and unfortunately, he happens to be a genius at it. These encounters are rare indeed. The one-night stand norm is a horny guy who thinks the best sex is going at it greedily and feigning passion. Telling that sort of lover to stop would be easy.

"How about we go in there?" Upton points toward my bedroom with his chin.

This decision has to be a quick one. I *could* lead him to paradise. I *want* to. But I've made up my mind about taking the road with Finn. I want to know more about the Zombie pills and the small towns that have been decimated by vampires. I choose *that* over *this*.

"I'm sorry, we can't," I whisper while the tips of our tongues taste each other.

He doesn't stop. "Why not?"

"Because."

"Because?"

"Because this is our first date," I say.

"But not our last."

The truth is the opposite, but I play along. "Then what's wrong with waiting?"

"Nothing at all, but we don't have to wait." His hand is back under my dress, and his finger gently presses against a very sensitive area under my panties.

"Whoa, Nelly," I say, guiding his hand away. Having his finger there gives him an unfair advantage. "Look, let's just wait, okay?" This time, I sound sterner.

He gives me one last kiss on. "All right then." He withdraws his hands.

The second he steps away from me, I sigh with regret. He gives me his business card and says he wants to have breakfast, lunch, or dinner soon, that he'll take whatever I give him. His eagerness is cute and endearing. I tell him I'll call him. We engage in one more indulgent kiss before he leaves.

I sit on the foot of my bed, wondering why I should be alone tonight in order to appease Finn. It would've been fun to spend the night rolling in bed with someone like Upton.

After I slip back into my nightdress, rage fills me. What was that nonsense with Finn all about anyway? Pounding on the door like a madman? Yelling in my head, which is a stunning reality. *The guy can speak into my head!* And he got me to make Upton stop. My date left, and the vampire got what he wanted without further explanation.

Fueled by fury, I darn near leap to my feet and stomp out of the bedroom, through the living room, and to my door. When I swing it open, there he stands.

"May I enter?" Finn asks. His shoulders are tense, and there's a nervous look in his eyes.

For the first time, I sense a vulnerability about him, which in turn extinguishes my rage. Calmly, I step back to let him come in.

"I wanted to warn you about the fog," he says as he walks past me.

"The fog?" I'm really baffled. "I don't want to

talk about fog. I want to know why you disturbed my date. I didn't even think you cared."

He faces me for a while. I can't determine what his expression says about his thoughts. He's such an enigma.

"Are you in love with him?" he finally asks.

What a strange question. "Do I have to be?" I ask, sort of tetchily.

"You should be."

I can hardly believe he just said that. "What are you, the moral police?"

He shrugs. "Old-fashioned, I guess."

I can't help but snarl. I hate self-righteous people. They're the reason for war and prejudice and everything bad that happens in this world and between mankind. I can hardly believe Finn is one of those people. "Old-fashioned? Great! Be old-fashioned for yourself"—I stab my finger at my chest—"not for me!" I hardly ever raise my voice, but I'm pissed. I'm disappointed that the reason he made me tell Upton no is because he's "old-fashioned," not because he wants me for himself.

"You're angry with me," he says as if he can hardly believe it.

"Are you kidding me?"

"No." Again, he manages to sound aloof.

"What are you? Some thousand-year-old vampire who called eccentrics who threatened your hypocritical, puritanical values witches and burned them at the stake? Or-or-or"—I don't even pause to breathe—"were you riding out on crusades with the Spanish Inquisition? Or—"

"No," he cuts me off before I can think of something else to accuse him of. "I'm not a thousand years old, and I don't hunt humans. I leave that up to their authorities."

I'm almost panting. All of a sudden, what I've been riled up about seems minuscule—especially since my mood stems from a minor broken heart. "Sorry if I went overboard."

He frowns and stares into my eyes as if he's trying to figure me out. "No apology necessary."

We're looking at each other. To say the tension has dissipated would be incorrect. He did judge me for wanting Upton, and I'm still not over that. I decide to let it go though. No need to harp on it.

I sigh. "What were you saying about the fog?"

"I've destroyed the tunnels leading to the lab. Cort can only get in by taking the surface at night or in the fog."

"And you believe he'll come in the fog instead of at night?" I ask.

"Yes, because he's working with the Shams, and he's with a coven that has cast a spell to keep me out of the fog."

"So what does that mean?"

"The spell doesn't work if I'm with you. They don't know that though, which puts us at an advantage." He lifts one side of his mouth into a sinister smirk. "They'll find out the hard way."

"Okay…" He's so strange. I just don't get him. "Well, what do want me to do about the fog?"

"Be ready to leave."

"But Cort said he'd be back in two days."

Finn shakes his head. "He knows my handiwork. He's going to empty that lab and kill those guys you care so much about as soon as he can. It'll be bright and early in the morning. You can count on it."

I nod. What next? I don't know what comes next. "Okay." I feel as though I have to ask questions to keep us from falling into an awkward silence. "Do I pack a bag? Clothes, toothbrush?"

"A small one."

"Do I need money?"

"I have enough."

"Right, you're old-fashioned."

I say that to gauge his reaction, but he doesn't

react right away. He just watches me with puckered brows. Then he steps forward until he's only a few inches away from me.

"Glo," he says in a formal voice.

I'm confused. "Finn?"

"Thank you."

"You're welcome." I'm not exactly sure what he just thanked me for, but that's the note he leaves on.

CHAPTER 5
ĤIT THE ROAD

L ast night, I went to sleep the second my head hit the pillow. Even though I couldn't get Finn out of my head, I was physically and mentally drained. Yesterday had been a very *long* day. Right now, it seems like a bizarre dream.

The air in my apartment is ice cold, even as I lie wrapped in my sheets and blankets. Maybe I forgot to turn up the heater last night. This is not the time of year to forget to do that. So to stop my teeth from chattering, I count to five, throw the covers off of me, and run down the short hallway to the thermometer to set it to eighty degrees.

I'm taken aback. The heat is on and set to the right temperature. I walk over to the vent at the end of the hallway and stretch my arm to feel if warm air is flowing out of it. *It is.*

Out of my peripheral vision, I catch sight of what's beyond the tall windows in the living room. I've never seen anything like it. The fog is so thick I can't see an inch into it. I'm so mesmerized that as my feet move toward the window, I forget that my blood is turning into ice. I can hardly believe what I'm seeing. It's the fog Finn mentioned. This validates everything he said last night. This is actually happening.

"I see you're not prepared," Finn says.

At first I think he's doing the telepathic thing, but when I whip around, he's standing behind me. I jump, startled. "How did you get in here?"

"You're cold." Finn walks up and wraps his arms around me.

In less than a second, I go from being icy cold to full-on warm. "Wow."

"I notice this happens when we touch," he says.

"Then you feel it, too?" I ask.

"I do."

This effect must stem from us being bonded. I should probably mention that fact, but after last night, it would just make the nature of our association much more confusing.

"Yeah," I say. I'm just now realizing how my entire body is throbbing because not only he's warm, but every part of his body is hard—*every part.*

"It's time we head out. You should get yourself ready," he says with his mouth very close to my ear.

I look down at his hands, which are pressed against my abdomen. He hasn't loosened his grip on me yet. Truth be told, I don't want him to. "I would but…" I keep looking at his hands.

He releases me. The moment he lets go of me, the cold air latches on to my skin. When I turn around to give him a final look before heading off to get dressed, he's watching me with his eyes ablaze with lust. I step around him and allow my weak knees to carry me to the bedroom, where I slip out of my red nightdress and fold it into a black leather overnight bag.

I'm the queen of packing light. I work quickly, folding clean underwear, a heavy pair of jeans, and two thick sweaters into the bag. I brush my teeth and shove the toothbrush and paste into the carrier. I splash water over my face and pat my skin dry with a thick, soft black towel. Without intending to, I end up staring at my reflection. Indeed, I have Finn's eyes.

"Glo," he calls. "It's time to go."

"Okay," I shout over my shoulder.

The last thing I do is slip into a pair of jeans and a gray fitted sweater. I slip on a thick pair of socks and a pair of gray leather UGG boots; I think they're the warmest brand out there. I give my bedroom the final once-over. I don't know when I'll be back; something tells me it won't be soon. When I walk into the living room, carrying my bag, Finn doesn't speak. The way he's looking at me says it all.

"Almost all ready," I say. I go over to the closet, take out my gray wool pea coat, and slip it on. "Now I'm ready."

He holds the door open for me. I guess that's his way of saying, "Let's go," so I take one deep sigh and do as he wishes. Unlike myself, Finn doesn't take the stairs to the lobby; he takes the elevator. Unfortunately, this gives the nosy neighbor with a profound crush on him time to rush out of her apartment and wait for the doors to slide open alongside us.

"Good morning," she says to Finn, batting her eyelashes and grinning.

He scowls at her for a brief second then stares straight ahead. The poor girl's mouth falls open, and she turns beet red as if she's been slapped on both cheeks, her forehead, and her chin. Finn is either unaffected by how his disregard for her has made her feel, or he's oblivious to it. Actually, I'm pretty sure it's both.

She glances at me. I lift my eyebrows, taking pity on her. If she knew what he really is, then his reaction would probably make more sense. With the way he looks, I imagine he's used to bold advances from women. Things get worse when the elevator arrives. The doors slide open, and Upton is standing inside. He's winded, staring at me and only me.

"Glo," Upton says, still huffing and puffing.

"Upton?" I say, shocked to see him. "Are you okay?"

"I had to run to keep from freezing my ass off. It's bloody cold outside. But we have to talk. Could we talk?"

Finn steps into the elevator as the neighbor girl, who is in her early twenties, digs through her brown Coach bag as if she's forgotten something. I know she's only pretending. At the moment, I'm caught between three emotions: shock at seeing Upton, pity for her, and urgency because of Finn glaring at me. Before I can follow him into the elevator, Upton steps out and takes me by the waist.

"How about we go back to your flat and have a chat?" His eyes beg me to oblige him.

"Glo," Finn barks, standing at the back of the elevator. He expects me to enter and be quick about it.

I'm undecided as I look between both men. I don't want to be rude to Upton.

"I'm sorry, are you engaged at the moment?" Upton asks as he acknowledges Finn.

I gently wiggle out of Upton's grasp, take his hand, and lead him into the elevator with me. The neighbor is already heading back to her apartment, shamefaced and still digging through her bag.

As the doors slide closed, I turn to Upton. "Listen, I'm going to be gone for a while."

Upton leans forward to look around me. "Aren't you the bloke from the party?"

Finn doesn't answer. He stares straight ahead, appearing to grow angrier by the second.

"Yes," I answer for him.

"Are you related?" Upton asks me.

That's when Finn turns to stare daggers at us. Even *I* jump out of my skin. Upton quickly takes his eyes off of him and keeps them on me.

"Well…" It's time to lie again. "Yes, we are. Some serious family business has come up, so we have to attend to it." All of that tumbles out of my mouth like bad lies do.

Finn says, "No, we're not related."

Upton narrows his eyes in confusion. "You're not?"

"Yes, we are." I give Finn a look that warns him to stay out of it. "He's just grouchy right now. My cousin. We're not that close but..."

The doors slide open, and Finn stomps into the lobby. "Keep up."

His demeanor makes it easy for Upton to believe my story. The lie was for Upton's own good —and mine, of course.

"When will you return?" Upton asks.

We're both trying to keep up with Finn, who pushes the glass door open with his back and stands there waiting for me to come along.

"I'll call you," I say as I trot over to Finn.

With one last glance at Upton, I step out into the fog. Confusion and disappointment colors his face. I sigh with regret. It hurts to see him that way, but I'm unable to let guilt affect me for too long. It's *literally* ice cold out here. The vapors are so thick, I can't even see Finn.

"What the hell?" I mutter and wrap my arms around my chest. "I can't see anything."

"Why not?" Finn asks from somewhere in front of me. He still sounds crabby.

"I just can't," I snap.

"How do you see through walls?"

I feel my eyebrows knit together as I think. I get it—I have to use my second sight. I tell myself that I want to see through the fog, and miraculously, it happens. The day is almost clear again. It's strange —I can see that the fog is still here, but it's gone at the same time!

Finn has stopped to observe me. Once he's sure I've adjusted, he continues leading me down a long alley. We reach a metal garage door on the building to the right. I can't stop myself from shivering as Finn yanks the padlock open. The chill goes right through my clothes, as if I'm standing here wearing nothing at all. Finn takes one of my hands, instantly warming me.

"Thank you," I whisper. My throat has yet to recover.

"Next time, take my hand. Don't stand there and freeze to death."

His tone could be construed as harsh, but by now, I understand him enough to know that's his general tone. I nod and let his words roll off my back.

He walks me over to the passenger-side door of a huge black truck. The huge black cover over the bed makes it look like an SUV, but it's not. Once I crawl into the passenger seat, he lets go of my hand. Before I can fully turn to my left, he's in the driver seat, and the engine is on.

How can someone move that fast?

Finn reaches out for my hand again as he guides the vehicle out of the compact garage. I take his without hesitating. It's too cold to pay attention to how every time we touch skin to skin, my heart flutters.

Not a soul is walking the sidewalks, and there's hardly any traffic other than a few buses with "Out of Service" lights on. I see one cab, and it's driving slowly. Not Finn though. He's barreling down the road, taking full advantage of the current traffic conditions. I gaze out the window, looking inside buildings. One would think this was a ghost city if it weren't for a couple of customers in the Spruce City Café and a few in Union Bank. As we speed up Payne Avenue, I see one person bundled up so thick that he or she looks like an Eskimo.

"When we get there, what do we do?" I ask, remembering that I'm not alone.

"We wait," Finn replies.

"And then what?"

"We follow him."

Finn is leaving out an entire middle part of the story. *Deliberately*.

"What about the men? The chemists?"

He pauses for so long that I think he's choosing to ignore me. Finn's real good at choosing not to answer questions. I'm about to ask him again when…

"They chose their fate," he says.

"What does that mean?" It sounds to me that he's going to let something bad happen to them.

"Those guys knew they were dealing with vampires. Now they have to face the consequences."

I think about that as Finn stops the truck alongside a curb. We're two blocks north of the empty lot and the shelter. However, it's clear why Finn picked this spot. From here, we have a clear line of sight to the lot.

"It's that cut and dry to you, isn't it?" I finally ask him.

"It is."

"What about the girl?" I ask, totally off subject.

"Which girl are you referring to?"

"The neighbor girl."

"What about her?" Finn's expression is even more pinched than it was a second ago.

"Didn't you care that you hurt her feelings?"

"No." Again, he's blunt.

"And you don't care if those guys are killed either?"

"No."

I stare into his face, searching for a hint of compassion. "I thought all vampires were human at one point in their lives." I pick his expression apart with my eyes.

He observes me just as curiously as I study him. His lips are pressed tightly together, and I'm pretty sure he has no reply to my last statement. I let out a deep sigh, figuring his inability to feel is probably the reason why we're bonded. I'm the one who has to care about the lives of others if he's unable to.

So far, Cort hasn't shown up. I could go in and warn the chemists. Let them know that today may be the last day of their lives. Just thinking about that possibility makes my heart beat too hard.

"I'm going in," I mutter. I hop out of the truck and into the bitter cold fog. Before I can take my first step, Finn is in front of me, blocking my forward progress. I try to push past him. "Move!"

He doesn't budge an inch. "Is that all you're going to use on me? Is that your biggest weapon?"

I flinch, taken aback. That sounded like a challenge. "You want me to burn you?"

"That's the only way you're getting around me."

We engage in an epic stare-down. I'm really considering lighting him up. I don't have to kill him, just incapacitate him.

"You *will* have to kill me," he assures me.

"What, you can read my mind?"

"No. I just know what you're thinking."

I think about my chances. I'd have to leave him sizzling in pain in order to reach the building, get inside, and run to the basement without being stopped. A lot could go wrong on my way to save two people. I may end up hurting more people in the process. So I sigh, giving up.

"Why can't we help them together?" I ask.

"Those men have to hand over the Zombies. Cort has to think he's getting away scot-free."

"And there's nothing we can do?" I'm pleading with him to find a solution, any solution. "They may be working for vampires, but they have families. Someone will care if they end up dead."

Finn watches me, perplexed. I'm shivering

again, so he puts his hands on my shoulders. He still keeps the same expression on his face.

Ah, there's the warmth, chasing away the cold.

"Wait inside the truck," he mutters.

A smile spreads across my lips. I can tell by his tone that he's going to attempt to save their lives. My outward display of joy makes him frown even harder. Then his fingers slide down the corner of my mouth. He's gone before I can fully react to his sensual gesture.

I climb back into the warm cab to watch what's going on in the lab. Three chemists are present this morning. They're busy as bees mixing chemicals, stirring, and pouring them. Not one of them looks up from their work until Finn appears in the room. I just now notice that he's wearing black pants and a long-sleeved black T-shirt. His outfit is very ninja-esque, and there's a stark contrast between the black clothes and his very pale skin and eyes. The chemists have no doubt about what he is. One of them even drops a beaker. Clear liquid and glass splatters all over the floor.

"If you choose to stay, you'll die. Get out now," Finn says.

All three people in biohazard suits turn to look at each other. By the time they turn back to face

Finn, he's gone. Three seconds later, he's sitting next to me.

"There," he says.

"That's it?" I thought he'd do more than that.

"That's all they need if they value their lives," Finn mutters as he looks on.

Strangely enough, I get where he's coming from. They could tell he was a vampire warning them to get out. If they choose to stay, and consequences are suffered, then it's their fault. I sit on the edge of my seat, watching the men peel out of their plastic white suits.

"What about the Zombies?" one guy asks another.

"Leave them."

"What about the money, man?" the third guy says. "He's supposed to pay us today."

"Didn't you hear what he said? They're going to kill us."

"Who the hell was he anyway? I ain't ever seen him before. Have you?" the one who's concerned about getting paid asks.

"No, but I'm getting the hell out of here." The second chemist kicks his suit against the wall and darn near runs out of there.

"Come on," I mutter, studying the other two chemists. "Leave."

"Get ready for a lesson in humanity," Finn whispers.

I glance at him.

Back in the lab, the guy who's concerned about the money says, "You can go, but I'm staying."

The first guy looks torn.

"Maybe I should go in there," I say.

"Absolutely not," Finn roars. "It's their choice. They've been warned." He widens his beautiful eyes. "That's more than I ever do."

We're compromising. He's given me what I wanted, and now I have to step back and let him do his job.

"There he goes," Finn announces excitedly.

I follow his line of sight through flat buildings and see a cream Mercedes Benz equipped with all the bells and whistles. I look past the black tinted windows and see Cort. He's not alone. There's a female with very long dark hair with him. Her chocolate-brown eyes are shaped in a way that makes her look as if she just woke up. She's wearing skintight jeans and heels that are least four inches high.

"Tal," Finn growls.

"Who is she?" I watch as they both flow out the shiny luxury car.

"She's a Sham."

Tal lifts her arms and turns in a circle.

"What is she doing?" I ask.

"Looking for *me*."

I want to glance at him, but I can't take my eyes off Cort and Tal. They walk with their backs straight, and their strides are long. They appear entitled as they stroll through the front entrance of the homeless shelter.

The shelter is bursting at the seams, being that the outside has turned into a foggy deep freezer. The staff rushes up and down the hallways, trying to get people checked in. No one really pays attention to the two vampires. Tal turns up her nose as she strolls past people in soiled and over-worn clothes, waiting to be assigned a bed for the day.

"Damn putrid humans," she hisses.

Cort doesn't react. He walks quickly with an intense expression. Finally, he looks to the right. "Him and him." Cort points at two men.

Tal flicks her fingers at both men, and they follow without question.

"Who are they?" I ask Finn.

"The puppets," Finn says.

I stare at him, wondering what that means.

He must be able to read the look on my face through his peripheral vision because he says, "They're impressionable."

"What makes them so impressionable?"

"It's the scent of their souls."

"Vampires can smell souls?" I ask.

"Not *vampires*. He can, and she can."

"But they're vampires, aren't they?"

Finn glances at me. "They're a new breed. That's why they can smell souls. They can also drink vampires like me and live. Another reason why they have to die." He says this so casually. It's clear that this is his life and has been for a very long time.

I watch Cort and Tal lead the two tattered men deep underground.

"So what happens to them?" I ask. "The two homeless guys?"

"They'll be killed."

"And you don't care about them either, I presume?"

"Am I supposed to?"

"If you can do something about it, then yes!"

Finn sighs and frowns, as if the act caught him

off guard. "Damn, haven't done that in a long time."

"What, sigh?" My face feels tense. I'm still irritated by how nonchalant he is about people dying.

"Yes. Never had to until you came along."

"That's because you're heartless, and I'm not. If we're going to be 'bonded,' then you can't be this way. I won't stand for it. And really—who made you God? A rotting bush can sprout roses with a little tender loving care." This has always been my philosophy with unsavory people. "Shouldn't they get a chance to smell like a rose?"

Finn keeps his eyes forward. He's remaining silent, which is fine. I won't push him as long as he hears me and gives my words some thought. However, I'm anxious down to my bones. I can run fast if I want but not as fast as Finn. The element of surprise is the key to beating him. The only downside to my plan is that I'll have to burn him a little. I don't want to do that.

"The tunnels," Finn whispers, interrupting my thoughts.

I snap my eyes to him. "What about them?"

"I collapsed them from the apartment," he says and stares into my eyes as if he's just given me a hint. "If I can do it, you can do it."

"You're saying I should use my power from right here?"

"But wait for the right moment. You have to watch and feel for it," he says.

My heart is beating so fast. I feel Finn staring at me as I keep my eyes on the scene. My brain is on standby, waiting to give my eyes the order.

Tal and Cort stroll into the lab with their chests high and heads high. Everyone knows they're in control. The two chemists in biohazard suits stop working to acknowledge them. Although they appear to be the picture of calm, they're not. The one chemist's hands are shaking, and his knees are knocking. He's the one who questioned whether to go or stay. The other chemist, who was concerned about being paid, is more in control of his fear. He puts his hand on a pistol in the hip pocket of his biohazard suit-coat.

"Can they be shot dead?" I ask Finn.

"No," he answers.

"Stop, stop. Whatever you're doing, stop," Cort sings in a dark tone. "Off with the beekeeper suits."

The two chemists turn to face each other. Now they're worried.

"Take them off," Cort shouts because they're not moving fast enough.

I could set him on fire right now and not flinch. I can't believe how much I *want* to harm him. I know whatever he has planned for the two men is horrific.

The chemists practically tear themselves out of their safety gear. The one with the gun knows his protection is on the floor, and his eyes are glued to it. I imagine he's wondering how to retrieve it.

"Go ahead," Tal says to him while standing behind Cort. The way she grins makes her look like the Joker from Batman. "Pick it up." She has an Eastern European accent.

"I don't know what you're talking about," the chemist says.

In a blink of an eye, her hands are around his throat, choking him so hard that his eyes look as though they're bulging out of the sockets. He doesn't even have enough air to gag. As soon as she lets go, he withers to the floor, coughing to regain his breaths.

"Get. The. Gun," she demands, not even compassionate enough to let him catch his breath.

Finally, he's scared. Like his partner, his hands are too jittery to retrieve the pistol fast enough for Tal. Before we all know it, Tal has gone into the pocket and set the gun on the blacktop lab table.

"Pick it up and aim it at him." She tilts her head toward his partner.

The foolishly brave chemist's hands are raised, and he's shaking in his boots.

"Take it!" she shouts, looking and sounding deranged.

He fumbles the gun off the table and points it at his lab partner. The firearm shakes in his hand. The other chemist pleads for his life.

"Kill him!" Tal commands.

"Wait," Cort shouts. "That's my lead scientist, you insane bitch!" He takes the gun out of the man's hand and puts it in the lead chemist's hand.

I get angrier by the moment.

"Before you kill him, Jung, where are my Zombies?" Cort asks.

Now the gun is shaking in Jung's hand. "I don't want to kill anybody!"

"The Zombies," Cort insists.

Jung tilts his head to the right. "There in the bin."

Cort looks over at it. He looks relieved. "How many?"

"Two fifty."

"I said three hundred."

Tal exaggerates a yawn. Cort glares at her.

"Give us until tomorrow," Jung pleads feebly. "We'll have them then."

"Do you think I was born yesterday?"

"No," Jung says, trying not to piss off Cort more than he already has.

"Of course not, I'm a vampire! Why don't you turn that gun on yourself, then?" he says.

"I've seen enough," Finn says. "I know when the right moment arrives, and this is it. Do it, Glo."

My brain tells my eyes to make the gun too hot to hold. Jung drops it and squeezes his burned hand. That was easy enough.

Cort yells, "Pick it up!"

Tal's eyes dart around the room. I keep my eyes on both of the vampires, and I imagine them charring in the flames of a raging furnace. They hug themselves, shrieking in pain.

"Don't kill them," Finn warns me. "Not yet," he mutters as he watches them intensely.

I turn down the fire in my head. Although they're not burning to death, they still feel the heat. Jung and his partner look confused as Cort and Tal roll on the floor, trying to put out the flames.

"Why aren't they leaving?" I ask.

"It takes them a while," Finn mutters.

Smoke is rising from the vampires' skin. Finally,

Jung and the other chemist shake themselves out of their stupor. They hesitate, as if they don't know whether they should escape or not, before the second chemist just goes for it. He takes off in an all-out sprint, and Jung allows himself to follow.

Through my upward peripheral vision, I can see that the two homeless men have come to themselves since my power broke Tal's spell over them. They're befuddled, roaming around the tiny vestibule outside of the lab.

"Damn, they're not leaving," I say under my breath.

I hear a door slam, but I dare not look toward it for fear of losing control of the intensity I'm inflicting on Cort and Tal. All I can ascertain is that Finn has left the car. I see him on the threshold, waving the two homeless men toward him. To my relief, they follow his lead, but both stop when they hear Tal scream as her head erupts into flames. Cort wails as his legs ignite.

I squirm because I don't know how to keep them quiet. The two vampires are on fire, and Finn has asked me not to kill them. The two homeless men are on the verge of attempting to rescue them without realizing the danger. Finn races over to grab both men before they can bolt into the lab. In seconds, all three of them are up the stairs and out of the basement.

That's when I let go of the fire. I'm panting as if I've just finished running a marathon at top speed. My arms and legs, my entire body feels as if something or someone very heavy is pressing upon me, and my head is spinning like a top. How I'm feeling isn't normal. I think I'm about to faint. The last thing I see is Finn's pinched expression. I faintly hear him ask me if I'm okay, then everything goes white.

There's light. It's so thick that even when I try to see through it, I can't. I'm pretty sure I'm conscious. I feel as if I am, but where's Finn?

"Glo," someone calls. His is an unfamiliar voice. "Open your eyes."

I think my eyes are already open; I'm struggling to see past the light. I grunt. My head aches from pushing my sight to new limits.

"Relax, Glo," he whispers in a soft, stern tone.

I suck in a deep breath, and I don't know if I'm breathing on my own anymore. What's clear is that after he said to relax, I did.

"You're the fifth daughter of the House of Benel. You're visible now, and I give you my protection," he says.

All of a sudden, the light surrounding me penetrates me. I'm swallowing it. I'm breathing it. It's flowing into my pores. The ache in my head is gone. Am I floating? I think I am. Is the day perfect and warm? I feel as though I'm sunbathing on a beach in Naxos, Greece, during the height of summer.

Warm hands are on my face. "Glo," a familiar, panicked voice calls. "Wake up, Glo."

Now I know for sure that my eyes are closed. When I lift my lids, Finn's face is right above mine. I'm lying on a small bed in the back part of the truck cab. The only light flows in from the windshield, and it's dim. I push myself up to sit.

"Whoa, slow down," Finn warns.

I turn to look out the front window. It's night. The only light comes from a lamppost along the side of the road.

"What happened?" I ask.

"You've been asleep for the last six hours, but just now you lit up."

"I lit up?" I ask, confused.

"Yes. You had light coming out of you."

Just like in my dream? Or was it real? "Was there a man here?"

He frowns while looking into my eyes. "No. But

—you were glowing. Then I started glowing. Then the truck. What the hell's going on?"

"I have no idea," I whisper, thoroughly confused. "Where are Cort and Tal?" My voice is still drowsy.

"Just stay here and lie down," Finn whispers.

We blink at each other. My heart races because he appears to be on the verge of doing something I thought he'd never do. His eyes pan from my face down to my toes. He places his hand on my abdomen, and it dawns on me that he can see my skin through my sweater. A low guttural rumble fills the cab.

"Finn?" I ask, wondering if he's going to be okay.

"I'm sorry," he whispers. "It's…" He lifts the hem of my sweater, and his hands caress my belly. What a gentle touch he has. He acts almost as if he's discovering skin for the first time. "What are you made of? You're not flesh."

My mouth is caught agape. I'm not surprised by what he just said; I can't get over how out-of-this-world divine his hand feels. Upton had a fantastic touch, but Finn's… I can hardly explain it.

He lifts my sweater. He hesitates and glances into my eyes before continuing pulling it up until my nipples, which are standing firm in my red satin bra, are exposed. He's studying my breasts as if they're the most interesting portrait in the art gallery.

"May I?" he whispers, looking into my eyes.

My voice cracks as I say, "Yes."

He slides a finger around one hard nipple before he pulls down the material covering it. A growl escapes his throat. His two fangs grow right before my eyes. I wonder if he's going to bite me. I would let him if he wants to. I would give in to him one hundred percent. Instead, he lowers his mouth to my nipple, and his warm tongue makes the nerves inside it tingle. I'm panting. His lips, tongue, and teeth work in unison to make me throb all over.

"What are you?" he whispers.

I'm unable to say a word. As his lips slide up my neck to my mouth, his hands massage my breasts. After his tongue tastes mine, he crimps his brows. I hate that he stopped; my entire body aches for more of him. I want him to enter me, but he's far away from that. I'm still wearing pants, and although I can feel how hard he is, he's fully dressed. Usually when guys get to the point he's at now, they can't get their pants unzipped fast enough. But not Finn. He's in discovery mode. I wonder if he's a virgin. *No way*. Or maybe, like he said, he's just old-fashioned and is fighting against his lust.

He nibbles my chin as his hands slide back down my stomach and into my pants to touch me *there*. His eyes get that blazing look they have when he gazes at me sometimes. Like last night in the hallway before he pulled me into his apartment. One of his fingers slides inside me, which for sure is a move far beyond a virgin's skill set. Only an expert can make me close my eyes like this and give in to a moan.

He stops.

I open my eyes.

He's staring at my face with that conflicted look again.

I can't believe I'm about to say this. "Finn, don't do anything you're uncomfortable with. I know you're old-fashioned and—"

"I'm what?" He appears a bit bothered by what I said, but not enough to take his fingers out of me.

I let out a breath. "Huh?" *What did I just say?* "Oh, you're old-fashioned."

"Only in that if I want you, I want you to only want me."

"Oh." I do only want him. Ever since the day I laid eyes on him, I've only wanted him.

He kisses my lips again. Everything his mouth does, the tip of his tongue does too. "You taste so damn good. I wonder…"

The next thing I know, my boots and jeans are off and lying on the floor beside me. His mouth is right above where his fingers used to be.

I let out a loud gasp as his tongue works my pleasure spot. I can't stop moaning and whimpering, and I wonder if this is really happening. All guys do this but never like this. When I look down at him, Finn's looking up at me, studying my face. I let out a loud, uncontained cry of pleasure when I come. After another swift move, he's inside me *finally*.

We're kissing, and I think I'm crying from the frustration of him being deep inside me but not deep enough. He thrusts skillfully. He knows where to guide himself, knows what I should feel when he gets there. When I come again, so does he. When I cry out, he growls. He wraps his arms around me, holding me tightly.

Everything is silent and still around us. I know we're somewhere in the middle of nowhere. I don't want to be the first one to speak and risk ruining the moment. What we did was epic, and we were still half-dressed. It was a true journey into the sensual.

"I don't know how to stop wanting you," he whispers.

I'm speechless. I don't *want* him to stop wanting me. He lifts up and looks me in the eyes. We gaze at each other before he thrusts again. This time, he moves much more slowly.

"What does this mean?" I ask.

"That I've given in to you."

"Is that good or bad?"

He lowers his face to curve the tip of his tongue around my left nipple. When my nipple is nice and wet, he kisses it dry before moving to the right one to do the same thing.

"Both," he answers after another moan escapes me.

CHAPTER 6
THE EMPTY TOWN

It was the strangest thing. Finn just stopped. In one whirlwind move, he slipped on his pants, zipped them, and stood over me.

"You can rest while I drive," he muttered.

And that was it.

Now, after changing my underwear, I lie on the bed, trying to figure out how to get past the awkwardness that now exists between us. I knew Finn was a bit strange, but I attributed that to him being a vampire. He's not Bram Stoker's Count Dracula or Anne Rice's Lestat, but neither is he Rice's Louis. Instead, he's like *that guy,* the one every girl has dated at least once, maybe twice if his stinger didn't hurt badly enough during round one. He's the most complicated being a girl will ever agree to get involved with. He slips and tells you he loves you, which makes him hate you. Probably because he grew up in his own version of *Mommie Dearest*. Or worse, he's the actual depiction of Conrad Jarrett in *Ordinary People* and a Beth Jarrett is his mother.

Basically, the woman he's supposed to love most in this world snubbed him, stripping him of all his trust in the female species, and now every woman he comes in contact with has to pay for it. Guys like that sink their claws in us by giving us glimpses of their deep, dark, broken hearts, and all we want to do is fix the unfixable.

I'm kicking myself for crossing that line. Why did I let him make *emotional* love to me? I should've known better. Now I'm going to have to pay for it. That's if I let him dump on me.

I kick the thick covers off of me. There are four heavy blankets on this bed. He must have laid them over me after I fainted as a way to show his "concern." I don't need him taking care of me with one hand and then stabbing me with both hands.

I sit up and look around. There are no windows back here, but I can see that we're speeding down an unlit two-lane highway with tall bushy trees lining both sides of the road. The sky holds thick, gray and white cumulus clouds. The snow on the ground is melting away, and we zoom across a small bridge with a half-frozen creek slogging along beneath it. I have a feeling we're heading south.

I knock on the window that separates the front of the truck from the back. The glass slides open.

"What?" he asks. His voice is cold and disengaged, which proves my theory. This vampire has serious mommy issues.

"Where are we going?" My tone is just as chilling, which makes him do a double take in the rearview mirror.

"Lo Creek, Alabama." This time he sounds less rude—on purpose of course.

"Watch out," I say. Before he can object, I crawl through the window separating us.

Finn looks shocked, but I don't care. If he needs all business because he can't handle more, then that's what I'll give him. What we did was fun. I've had plenty of that type of fun since my supernatural friend is an international party addict. Upton wasn't the first guy I got involved with after one of Aries's soirées, and after this whole escapade with Finn is over, he won't be the last.

I latch my seatbelt and settle my buttocks

comfortably in the seat. "Okay now, why are we going to Lo Creek, Alabama?"

He hesitates. "It's Cort's next target town."

"What do we know about this place?"

He frowns harder and studies my serious expression. It's amazing how he can drive without looking at the road.

"Nothing until we get there," he finally says.

I nod stiffly. "How far do we have to go?"

"About another hour."

"What will you do when the sun rises?"

He thumbs over his shoulder. "Stay back there."

"What will I do?"

I think he has no answer because he looks even more conflicted. I don't think he's completely factored me into the equation.

"You're used to going solo?" I say.

He remains silent.

I sigh hard. "Well, what would you do if you could go out in the daytime?" For one, two, three, four seconds, all I hear is the engine humming.

Then he says, "Find the dealer."

"What do you know about the dealer?"

"Nothing. I just know what one looks like."

"So you use your instincts."

"My knowledge," he asserts.

I flinch, taken aback. "Does that mean you think I have no knowledge?"

"No," he retorts. "I'm just more experienced than you are."

I scoff. "You think?"

He glances at me with knitted eyebrows. "Are you angry with me, Glo?"

"No," I snap. I'm furious with him and his mommy issues!

We fall silent for about fifteen minutes. I wonder what he's thinking. He must be thinking something because his eyebrows stay pinched the entire time. I'm thinking many things. I missed my coffee date with Aries this morning, and I wonder if she's called. I rummage through my bag that's still on the floor between the door and my foot.

Finn watches me take out my cell phone. It's been turned off, and I press the "On" button. As I wait for it to power up, I catch him shaking his head.

"What?" I snap.

"You're calling him already?"

"Him?" I ask, shocked. Who in the world is he talking about? "I'm not calling anyone. I'm checking to see if I have a message from Aries. We were supposed to have coffee, and I missed it. I don't want her to worry."

Only when the messages pop up and I see who most of them are from do I realize whom Finn was referring to. Three calls are from Upton and two from Lonnie, one of the waitresses from the diner. I'm sure she called to ask me to take one of her shifts. I have zero messages from Aries.

That's when my heart sinks. All of a sudden, I feel a cold breeze passing by my ears, and my head floats into space. Although Finn is sitting right next to me, he looks to be a hundred miles away. *I want to cry, want to cry, want to cry…* but don't cry. There must be an explanation for this.

I press number one, my speed dial number for Aries. "The number you have reached is no longer in service. Please hang up…"

I hang up.

This time I dial the actual number. Again, there's that annoying tone.

I hang up.

I dial Raz's number. The line rings once, twice, and then someone picks up.

"Bueno," a man says.

"Raz, is this you?" Desperation colors my tone.

"No," the man says. "I think you have wrong number."

"*Tres-uno-cero-cinco-cinco-cinco-tres-ocho-uno-uno*?"

"Si."

After my heart sinks, I mutter, "*Lo siento*." I hang up and look over my shoulder past the windowless shell attached to the back of the truck and down the road behind us. "I have to go back." The car hasn't turned around yet. "I have to go back!" I squeeze Finn's arm. "We have to go back! I have to go back!"

"Calm yourself, Glo. You're going mad."

"Don't you see? She's gone. She can't be gone. I have to look for her. I know I can find her. I just have to go home."

I feel the truck slowing a bit, but he doesn't stop.

"Who? Your friend?" He's nervous now.

I hate that I made him feel that way, but he doesn't understand. Aries is my life. She's all I have. The more I think about it, I can't help but cry. "She's gone. I know she's gone. I have to go back." I can hear myself sobbing. What will I go back to? Can we reset things? I close my eyes to get a hold of myself. Finn is right; I need to *calm down*.

"Glo?" His voice sounds so far away.

I feel the truck veer over to the side of the road and stop.

"Glo?" he asks again.

"She told me she would have to go away because I won't be hidden anymore." My eyes are still closed. All I want to see is her face. Then, I get an idea. My eyes pop open. I search and find the number for her office in my contacts list. After I dial it, I get the same message from the automatic operator. That's the confirmation—she's gone. I turn toward Finn. "I wanted to know everything, and now I'm all alone."

There's that conflicted look on his face again. Why am I trapped with such a love-challenged creature? I can't stand being alone with him.

I thumb over my shoulder. "I'm going to go back home. Good luck with everything." I reach for the door handle.

Finn grabs my arm and holds it. "Where do you think you're going?"

"I don't want to do this. I change my mind."

"I'm not going to let you walk back. You'll die out there."

"No, I won't. I'm not human, remember?"

He shakes his head. "This is insane. Stop this."

"Stop what? I just want to go back to my life."

Finn tightens his grip on my arm. "You can't do that anymore than I can go back to being human. It's over for us, Glo." As he looks me in the eyes, his other hand, the one that's not holding me, swipes the tears off one of my cheeks. "And you're not alone."

I swallow hard. He looks like he wants to kiss me, but I turn my face to gaze out the window. The world appears brand new with the way the melting snow weaves through the red-brown mud. There's a dark forest beyond the edge of the road, and I can see through it as if it's daytime. My eyes can change darkness into light and clear away all of that snow to see the ground dry. This is who I truly am.

Finn hasn't put the wheels back on the road yet. I don't care where I end up anymore. I think he's waiting for me to say something, but all I can remember is the light.

"While I was passed out, there was all of this light. You said you saw it." I wait for him to say something, but I refuse to look at him.

"Yes, I did."

"A man's voice told me that I have his protection. I think I know who he is. Someone named Felix Benel. My father."

"I heard your friend, Aries, mention him to you."

"That's right." I remember him acquiring that bit of information by blatantly eavesdropping.

During the silence, something happens. I can really feel Finn clutching my arm. He's no longer hundreds of miles away.

"You can take your hand off of me now," I finally say. "Let's just move forward."

"Look at me first."

I turn my head around to see him. He cups my chin in his powerful hand to study every part of my face. When I frown at him, he puts his hands back on the steering wheel. Finally, he puts us back on the road on our way to this place called Lo Creek.

As I stare out the passenger-side window, I ponder what the voice said while I was passed out. He said I have the protection with me. *If I wanted to, could I see it?* Just to cover all bases, my brain tells my eyes to look for it. So I do.

I gasp.

"Do you see it?" I ask Finn.

"See what?" He searches the rearview mirror to catch sight of whatever I might be referring to.

"It surrounds this truck. A…" I use my hand to gesture around us. "It's blue light. It's glowing."

Finn's brows are pinched as he tries to figure out what in the world I'm talking about. Then he flinches. "What the hell?"

"It's the protection. I wondered if it was there and if it could be seen, and there it is."

"I've seen this before," Finn says, studying the shield with wonder.

"You have?"

"I thought I saw it around your building on 6th Street before I set up there. I was looking for a place, and then it flashed. That's why I chose that building."

We stare at each other. I'm lost for words, and apparently he is too. The only thing I can think about is this bond we supposedly share. I still haven't seen any evidence of that—beyond the out-of-this-world sex we had not too long ago.

Finn turns away from me and continues driving. I study the glowing light and wonder how long it's been there. I let my mind play around a little by telling my eyes to see the protection and then not see it. Using my second sight makes me forget how depressed I am—and will probably be for the rest of my miserable life without Aries and even Raz— and I smile.

Finn sees me smiling and glances at me. Poor

thing. My emotional outbursts have put him on edge. To make him feel better, I withdraw into myself and stare out the passenger-side window again. The light disappears and reappears over and over as I tell myself to see it and then not see it. I find it amusing.

I wonder what else I can tell my eyes to do. I've only known them to be able to see through things and make things hot. Finn can shatter objects into a million pieces, so I focus on the snow-glazed leaves of the trees we pass.

Tear them, I tell my eyes.

Nothing happens.

Shake them.

The leaves rattle as though the trunks of the trees are being shaken. *That one I can do.* I turn to see if Finn saw. He's staring at me, and I guess he didn't see it.

"How can you do that?" I ask.

"Do what?"

"Look at me and drive without running off the road."

He snorts a chuckle. It's nice to see him do that. I like it when he's more sweet than sour.

"I can see in all directions at once."

"Get out of here!"

Again, he gives me that look as if he's trying to figure me out.

"What?"

"What?" he asks.

"What are you thinking when you look at me that way?"

"Look at you in what way?"

"When you were just looking at me, what were you thinking?" That question seems simple enough.

"You're beautiful, and—" He stops short.

"You're doing it again," I say, but I'm barely audible because I'm caught in his eyes.

"We'll arrive before sun-up," he says in a more formal tone. "I'll drive around and look into some places to see what sort of humans we're dealing with. They're not the gentlest species. If they're safe for you to be around, we'll get you a hotel room, and if they're not, then we'll hide out until sundown."

He's so weird. Even after saying all of that, he hasn't stopped staring at me in the way he does. What's even more bizarre is we're bolting ahead at ninety miles per hour, and the truck is perfectly between the lines.

THE CLOCK ON THE DASHBOARD FLASHES TWO A.M. when we drive past a tattered black sign that reads Lo Creek in faded white letters. Up ahead and to the right is a gas station. The lights are on above the island where the gas pumps are lined up and inside the flat, weather-beaten building that's dwarfed by the trees surrounding it.

Finn guides the truck up to one of the pumps and stops. "Do you want anything?" He opens the door, and cold air gushes in.

"No," I say, shaking my head.

I think he read my mind, though, because he'd already hurried out of his seat and shut the door behind him, stalling the chill seeping in. Finn puts the nozzle into the gas tank, and I hear the liquid filling it. When it clicks off, I watch him walk into the shop. He's such a magnificent specimen of a... vampire.

Once he's inside, I decide to stop gawking at him and survey the dark night. I picture all the trees as maniacal giants clutching clubs, arms raised and ready to pound the truck into the ground. I stretch my neck to search up the road, using my regular sight. I'm too afraid to use my second sight. I really don't want to discover anything scary. Not now.

That's when my peripheral vision picks up on

something white standing at the window to the right of me. I blink hard, thinking I'm seeing things. I shift my eyes a little to the right, and it's still there. After turning all the way around, I gasp and jump in my seat.

"Raz?" I shout, shocked and overjoyed. My hands fumble for the door handle, but before I can find it, he's in the cab of the truck next to me, which makes me jump again.

"Hey, Glo," he says in his usual draggy tone of voice.

"Where's Aries?" I search out the window, hoping his better half is somewhere out there. Finally it computes that he went from standing outside the window to sitting next to me in an instant. "Wait... How did you do that?"

"I'll tell you about it later. Finn is on his way back, and..." Raz gazes out the windshield and down the road. "This town is half-baked."

"Half-baked?" That's totally a Raz adjective. I'm glad he's still his old self. "But where's Aries?"

"I said I'll tell you later. Here he comes."

We watch Finn take a few normal, non-vampire steps out of the tiny building and stop not too far away from the entrance. He twists his head from left to right, searching in all directions.

When he flicks his face forward, he hurries back inside the truck at vampire speed. He always moves so fast, I can never hear the door open and close.

"I've seen you," Finn says, sitting on the opposite side of Raz.

"Yeah, I'm Raz."

Finn studies him as if he's trying to figure Raz out.

"He's a friend of mine," I chime in. "He and Aries…" My voice trails off as I search for her outside the windows again.

"She's not here," Raz assures me.

"Why are you here?" Finn asks.

Raz turns to me. "I'm what you call your Wek."

"Wek? I don't get it," I say.

"I watch out for you. When you were hidden, I made sure you stayed that way. Now that you're not, I'm your guide."

"I'm confused. Aren't you Aries's boyfriend?" I only realize how stupid that question is after I ask it.

Raz turns away from me; he looks impatient. "If it was your intention to move on up the road, then you should do it," he says to Finn.

Finn glances at me and then surveys our surroundings.

"What?" I ask Finn. He's acting as though something is wrong.

"I couldn't pay because there's no one inside even though the lights are on."

"He's in there," Raz counters. "He's hiding."

"Why?" I ask before Finn can.

"Because of the Selells."

"What the hell are Selells?" Finn looks frustrated.

"Vampires. You should move on," he tells Finn.

Finn and I catch each other's eye. I shrug, and he starts the engine and pulls out of the gas station. The farther we go, the more the trees give way to the tiny town. There's a simple white church with a big cross on the roof on my side of the road. The marquee reads Baptist Church. Behind it is a street lined with modest, flat houses. I see through the houses one by one. The porch lights are off, and they're all dark inside. Out of twelve homes, eleven are empty. The last has a woman sleeping fully dressed in bed with two kids, who are also clothed. They're all wearing sneakers, and a shotgun is propped up against the wall on each side of the headboard. I grunt curiously and turn to Raz and Finn.

Finn is searching the line of houses on the

opposite side of the road. "Did they take over this town already?"

"Not completely," Raz says.

"This is insane! There's a mother and her children lying there, scared to death. Why don't we just call the police?" I ask.

"There are no police here," Raz says. "Not anymore."

"Well, what's the nearest town? We'll call *their* police."

"Glo, *you*"—Raz thumbs over toward Finn— "and the slayer here *are* the cops. The only reason you got this far is because they can't see the truck past the protection. There's no getting in or out of this town."

I look at Finn to see if I can tell what he's thinking, but he's staring straight ahead. All I see is his sexy profile. I'm caught between admiring it and dreading our circumstances.

"When Selells can't get blood, what do they drink? Start there," Raz says. "And um, dude, when the sun rises, you don't have to go back there"—he tilts his head back toward Finn's dark sleeping area —"and hide if you stay inside the truck. The B&B on the other side of town is protected too." Then Raz disappears.

I shake my head. I can't believe how he and Aries lied to me for all of those years. My Wek? I've always loved Raz like a brother, even though he never said much. Sometimes we'd sit in the sand together, looking out over the ocean while Aries surfed or swam. We didn't have to say a word. We didn't even have to pretend to be wrapped up in what Aries was doing to pass through any awkward silence. Heck, I'd thought Raz was stoned half the time and tripping out in his head. It was only recently that I came to the conclusion that that's just the way he looks. Along with his draggy voice, he has sleepy eyes and shaggy hair, and he's very tan from being out in the sun all day. I always thought Raz's looks made him sexy, but at the same time, his peculiar behavior made him odd. He was the last person I would expect to be anything like a watcher or a guardian. I mean, really, am I in trouble?

"Hey," Finn says, trying to bring me back to Earth.

I was staring out the window as I thought. "Sorry, I'm here."

We're outside a place with the words The Shack painted in red on the sheet metal wall. A few cars are in the damp parking lot. I jump when thunder roars above my head. There's a flash of lightning, and then hail rains down, pounding the truck.

"What now?" I dread getting out of the warm cab and going inside.

"Look inside," he tells me.

I let myself see through the slush on the windshield and the wall of the structure. Although there aren't many cars in the parking lot, the place is pretty full. People are sitting at round tables that hold what look like empty wine and liquor bottles. There's no conversation, music, or dancing. These people are just guzzling drinks, glass after glass.

"That's a strange sight," I whisper.

"They're all vampires."

I study them closer. "They're pretty cosmopolitan for an out-in-the-middle-of-nowhere town like this."

"That's because they're not from here," Finn says.

"Well, why are they drinking so much?" I can't stop frowning at the scene. It's weird. Each vampire is focused only on their glass and the liquid inside it.

"They're parched. This is all they can do to soothe the thirst other than drink blood, which isn't easy to get."

"Yeah, I know." I sigh. "They can't drink human blood without permission. But then where is everyone? The townspeople?"

When Finn doesn't answer me, I glance at him. Once again, he's staring at me with *that* look.

"What?" I ask.

"I don't know where they are," he says, choosing to answer my first question.

I'm caught between a few thoughts. First, he still hasn't really told me why he looks at me in that way. It can't be because he finds me beautiful, can it? Second, I wonder why there are imported vampires in town. I can't get the picture of the mother sleeping in the bed with her children out of my head, and *that* thought trumps the other two.

"The mother," I say. "Do you think she can tell us anything?"

Finn shrugs. "I don't know. I never involve humans in vampire affairs." He focuses on what's happening inside the Shack. "I wonder where they go when the sun comes up."

"That's right," I mutter. "They're expendable."

He glances at me. "They're not expendable to me, Glo. Sometimes they're just a necessary sacrifice. You'll see."

I roll my eyes. "I hope not." It's clear we have different "slayer" values. But I'm curious, so I ask, "If I weren't here, what would you do to those vampires in there?"

"I don't have bloodlust," he says defensively. "I told you, I've got one purpose, and that's figuring out what Cort and whoever's backing him is doing. They're crossing lines too easily, and that's a problem."

"And then what?" I ask.

"Then I kill them," he says, just as calm as ever.

"I can't stop thinking about that mother. Do you think Cort needed the batch in two days to finish off this town?"

"Probably."

"Here's what else I think," I continue. "We should put as many people as we can find in that B&B. Then we should use me as bait."

"First part, maybe. If we find humans, we'll save them if they want it. Second part, *no*."

"Why not?"

"Because."

"Because?" I press him for a better explanation.

"This is why we shouldn't have done what we did," he snaps.

My mouth drops open. I feel as though I've been socked in the stomach. "What? Do you mean have sex?" I can't believe how sad I sound.

"It was more than that." He shakes his head. "We shouldn't have done it because…" He goes silent. This guy is *the* world's worst communicator.

"Don't worry, we won't do it again," I bark. I don't know why I'm so pissed.

I already knew that what we did was a huge problem for him, but it seems as though he's gotten worse. Will everything be blamed on the fact that Mr. Mommy Complex hates me but wants to screw me and possibly love me? Normally I wouldn't keep company with such a person, but now I have to. I scoff at the cruelty of fate.

When I look at him again, he's already staring at me. I'm through trying to figure out what that weird look means. It's time to get back to the issue at hand, starting at the point where we both agree. "Let's just get as many people to the B&B as we can."

He's still staring, but I keep my eyes forward, indicating that I'm ready to get on with the show. Finn starts the truck and, probably to settle me, goes straight to the house where the mother is sleeping with her children. I'm not surprised that he's right in front of me as soon as I scoot out of the truck. He doesn't want anything to happen to me. Apparently my life is the only one he's concerned about, and I don't find it at all flattering.

CHAPTER 7
ALL CAGED UP

Thick balls of hail pour down from the ashen sky. I knock on the door, not really expecting her to answer. As I look past the walls and through to her bedroom, I see the mother and the oldest kid, a girl who appears to be ten or eleven years old, each grab a shotgun.

I gaze at Finn with dread in my eyes. "This isn't going to be easy, is it?"

"No."

It's cold, so I fold my arms around my chest to warm myself. Out of nowhere, Finn grabs my hand. I glance at him.

"Thank you," I mutter as the shivering stops.

"You're welcome," he says, unable to take his eyes off the people in the house.

Past the wall, the little boy, who looks to be about five or six, is hiding under the bed. The young girl is standing a few steps behind the front door, aiming the shotgun. Her hands are shaking. The thick balls of hail pounding the roof do nothing to ease her nerves. The mother puts a finger to her mouth, telling the girl to remain silent.

I put my mouth close to the door and watch both of them closely. "Ma'am, I'm not here to hurt you! We're here to help!"

"Go away!" Her voice trembles.

"I can help!" I say louder.

"Go away!" she shouts.

The little girl's hands are shaking even more. I see her finger on the trigger while the barrel of her rifle is aimed right at my head. Without warning, their weapons turn to dust. I look into Finn's eyes, and they're glowing. He did it. Instead of being angry, I sigh with relief. I feared that at any second, that kid would panic and pull the trigger.

Finn nods as if to say, *this is how things work out here in the trenches.*

The door handle crumbles into powder. With the force of a cop tearing into a criminal's hideout, Finn shoves the door open. Unwanted chaos breaks out.

"Run!" the woman shouts at the girl, who takes off on command.

The woman cowers in the corner. Her wide eyes plead for her life as she faces Finn. Both children are under the bed, whimpering.

"What do you want from us?" she cries.

I step in front of Finn and lift my hands to appear less threatening; after all, he just kicked down the door.

"Ma'am, we just want to help," I say as gently as I can.

Her eyes dance between Finn and me. "Help how?" She has a strong regional accent.

I touch Finn's shoulder. "First, we need to get you and the children to a safe place."

She shakes her head. "I just don't know."

"Ma'am, what's been going on around here?" I take the opportunity to ask.

She scrutinizes us. "You don't know?"

"Not all of it. Here's what we do know. There are people down at the Shack who aren't your neighbors. All of *your* neighbors seem to be missing, but we're going to find them." I strongly believe Finn and I will get to the bottom of this.

Tears stream down the mother's cheek; she's

crying without even trying. "My husband…" She sobs. "They…"

I squat down beside her and wrap my arms around her. This is the saddest thing I've ever seen. Finn stares at us with that deeply confused look on his face again.

"Let's get you and your children out of here," I say.

After a brief hesitation, she nods. "Tammy, Sam," she calls.

Soon, her two wet-faced children appear. I take another look at their circumstances. For certain, this is the saddest thing I've ever seen.

As we walk under the pergola that covers the porch, I notice something. While Finn and I look directly at the truck, the mother and children search up and down the road. It dawns on me that they're unable to see the truck because of the protection. I touch the mother's shoulder and guide her as we all run straight ahead.

"Here," I say as I pull open the passenger-side door.

The entire family stops in their tracks as the inside of the truck becomes visible to them.

"Please, hurry and get in," I urge the mother. She still hesitates, so I say, "You can trust us."

She steps back. "Kids, go ahead."

They both file in. Finn is already inside, and he guides them over the seat to the back of the truck. The mother sits between Finn and me as we take off down the road.

"Ma'am—" I start.

"Suzanne," she corrects me in a deep Southern twang.

Suzanne's a tiny woman. She's almost a foot shorter than I am, which puts her at the high end of four feet tall. She's also slightly stout and probably in her mid-twenties. There's a youthfulness in her eyes that's buried deep under her distress, which is threatening to age her another twenty years.

"Suzanne, do you know if there are any more people here like you? You know, still human?"

She sighs. "What do you mean by 'still human'?"

Finn and I glance at each other. She must see the dread in *my* eyes at least, and her already weary face grows more worried.

"Nothing," I say, waving my hand dismissively. "Could you just tell us what happened here?"

"Well, it happened so fast." She sighs. "Teenagers were making noise in the streets, and Dell, my husband, went out to quiet them down.

Next thing we know, everybody's fighting. That's when I heard Dell shout code red."

"Code red?" What sort of family in a small town like this would ever think to have a *code red* signal?

"Well, yeah. If he says code red, then I'm supposed to gather the kids and lock ourselves in the panic room downstairs until it's all clear."

Finn glances at her. There's something in the way he looked at her—suspicion.

"You have a panic room?" I ask, hoping to draw out whatever piqued Finn's interest.

"My husband used to be a Navy Seal. He's not originally from around here." Her eyes grow dim. "He used to say these kinds of towns are danger in disguise. He only moved here because of me." Her voice cracks.

I don't want to push her any further, but I know I must. "Then what happened?"

"I got the kids, and we got down there as fast as we could. We waited for him forever. I grabbed a shotgun and came back up. Dell was gone. I knocked on all my neighbors' doors. Nobody was home."

"When did this happen?" Finn asks.

She focuses on him and crimps her brows as if

this is the first time she's really seen him. I know that look in her eyes—I had it when I first saw him. He *is* something to behold, even during times as such.

"The day before yesterday."

Finn looks disturbed by her words.

Up ahead, a blue light like the one that covers the truck extends from half of the road in front of the Southern Hospitality Bed & Breakfast to the back of the property. The truck rolls to a stop outside the front door.

"I'll go inside first and make sure it's safe," Finn says.

Once Finn steps outside, Suzanne's children crawl up front with us.

The little girl stares out the window and asks, "Is Daddy here?"

Suzanne curls an arm around her to comfort her. "I don't know, baby."

"He said he'd be back," the little boy says. He looks up at me. "Do you know where he is?"

The quick answer is the truth, which is no, but I see the trust in Suzanne's eyes. She believes I'm astute enough not to answer that question.

"*It's all clear,*" Finn says. He's speaking to me telepathically again.

"We can go inside now." I heave a small sigh of relief as we all scoot out of the truck and head up the sidewalk.

Walking under the protection is interesting. Beyond its borders, hail crashes hard against the ground, but standing on the sidewalk under the blue shield, there's no hail at all. The environment has been depleted of any temperature at all—it's neither hot nor cold.

We all marvel at this effect. Suzanne looks at me with questions in her eyes. The kids are so caught up that they drag along.

"Come on, hurry up," Suzanne urges them.

She stops to gather them to her, and they continue looking over their shoulders at the impossible as she moves them up the steps and into the B&B. Finn is waiting for us in the huge living room. He looks so out of place amongst the potted lilies, magnolias, and blue and pink orchids.

"Is anyone here?" I ask.

"No," he says.

I turn to Suzanne. "You'll be safe as long as you stay inside." At least that's what I hope.

She looks from me to Finn and nods. "I'm going to go find them a place to sleep, but I'll be back."

That's her way of letting us know she wants us to stay put because she has questions.

We watch the family drag up the stairs to the bedrooms. The little boy keeps looking back at us.

"Hey," Finn says to me as I stare up the empty stairwell. "I'm going to head back to the gas station. You'll be okay here?"

"Are you kidding me?" I ask.

He widens his eyes, appearing *so* aloof.

"We're a team, Finn, remember?"

Once again, he gives me his standard highly conflicted look.

"Why are you staring at me like that?" This time, I really want to know the answer.

"I'm used to being alone. That's all," he replies to my utter surprise.

"Me too," I confess.

He shakes his head. "No. No, you're not."

There's so much I want to know about him. Why is he so alone? How long has he been alone? Has he ever been in love? And how does he *really* feel about being bonded to me?

"But you're right," he says, shocking me again. "We're a team."

He moves swiftly, and he's standing right in front of me. Maybe it's because of his speed or because he's so close, but at the moment, I can hardly breathe.

Before Finn can speak, we hear, "What the hell was that?"

We turn to see Suzanne. She just saw Finn move at the speed of light. She hesitates before starting down the stairs.

"You were over there, and now you're right there," she says, pointing from the spot Finn just left to where he stands now.

"He's a vampire," I say, deciding to just come out with the truth.

Finn scowls. I don't think he feels telling her the truth is a good thing.

She steps back from us and clings to the banister. Fear fills her eyes when she barks, "A vampire? What the hell kind of games are you playing?"

I sigh with regret. Of course she doesn't believe me. I wouldn't believe me either. "Suzanne, what do you think has happened to your husband and everyone else in your town? They all seemed to vanish, right?"

She stares at me with parted lips. She's confused, but something flashes in her eyes, some glint of recognition. Then her eyes shift to the left and back. I can't help but be suspicious of her now. Did she just realize something?

Finn uses his speed to approach her at the base of the stairs. He opens his mouth to display his fangs. "She's right. I'm a vampire. I've been one for three hundred years, and I hunt other vampires. So does she. This is what's going on, like it or not."

"I-I…" She staggers another step away from him.

"I don't hunt humans, just vampires," Finn says, sensing her fears.

"What about you?" she asks me.

"I'm not a vampire." I leave out the fact that I'm not human either, which I still find preposterous. "And he's not going to harm you."

"What about…" She appears to be on the verge of crying. "What about Dell? My husband?"

"I don't know," I reply. "But we're trying to find him."

She digs in her jacket pocket, takes out a wallet, opens it, and slides out a photo. "Here." She hands the picture to Finn, who stares at it as if it's dung in his hands. "This is my husband. If you find him…" She swallows as she sniffs back tears. "Tell him I love him."

Finn turns sideways. Although he's not looking

directly at me, I know he's watching me. Without saying a word, he stuffs the photo into his pocket. In a nanosecond, he's standing at the door.

"Coming?" he grunts.

I nod and turn back to Suzanne. "Please stay inside. It's safe in here."

"I will," she promises.

All I can do is hope she keeps her word.

It's a little after three a.m. The sun will rise soon. I notice that the lights are on in just about all of the businesses, like the tiny market we just sped past and the hardware store across the street from it. There's a Hardee's, and the lights are on there too.

"I wonder why the lights are on," I say to myself.

"In case they missed one," Finn replies.

"So if someone runs in for help…"

"Then they're caught."

"Are you guessing, or is that a fact?" I ask.

"Experience," he says.

"Oh." I fall awkwardly silent. I can't oppose three hundred years of experience.

He pulls over to the side of the road. "Hey."

I'm already looking at him. "Hey."

"About what happened"—he thumbs over his shoulder—"back there between me and you?"

I sigh dismissively. "Don't worry about it. It's over."

"It's not over for me."

I flinch, taken aback. I watch his mouth, highly curious about what he's going to say next.

"I... Um, you're..."

As these words stumble past his lips, I think I'm holding my breath, so I let it out.

"It meant something to me," he confesses. "A lot."

I want to say that it meant a lot to me too, but I can't help but remain cautious. I still believe he has mommy issues. So I barely say, "Thank you."

"For what?" he asks to my surprise.

I'd thought my last response was me letting us both off the hook. "For saying that it meant more to you than what it was."

"I can love you," he whispers.

I blink, shocked by this revelation. "Oh."

I'm turning his words over in my head when all of a sudden, his lips are on mine, and his warm tongue presses against mine. His hands caress me freely. I love the way he kisses and gropes me. He knows how to do it with passion and not greed. His lips and tongue are slow, exploratory, as though he's taking his time to really figure out what I taste like.

"So," I say after we part lips, "do you remember your mother?" It's so silly of me to ask that, but I've already said it, so I wait for an answer.

"Yes. Why?" He's frowning, seemingly confused about why I would ask such a thing.

"Was she nice?"

After a moment, he lets out the loudest laugh. I didn't think Finn had it in him to laugh that hard. I watch him, fueled by both curiosity and fascination.

"Yeah, she was nice," he says, grinning as he drives again.

When the moment passes, I want to shrink into my seat. Does he know what I was insinuating? Other than being embarrassed, I'm floating on cloud nine. His taste is still on my lips. The heat his kiss generated is still there too.

I'm pretty sure he likes me a lot, especially when he takes my hand. That one action reassures me that I didn't offend him by asking about his mother. My heart is seriously pounding as my eyes widen. This is no mediocre handholding. It's full-on woven fingers contact. I can hardly take it.

I'm still trying to keep myself from panting as the truck pulls into the driveway of the gas station and stops in front of the door. As soon as the truck stops, Finn pulls me to him and kisses me again. He's getting bold about it, and I love it! I'm dizzy by the time his tongue and teeth take the last taste of my top lip. *He's so sensual.*

"Are you ready?" he whispers, still leaning toward me.

All I'm able to do is nod.

"I would kiss you again," he says, "but..." He glances toward the back of his truck where the bed is.

I smirk, and he smirks back. We get out of the truck and enter the small convenience store. I'm on guard, and I know Finn is too. We tread past the refrigerated products, such as beer, ice cream, soda, water, and milk. I'm following Finn, but it doesn't make sense to shadow him. We're supposed to be a duo, so I force myself to branch off and start down an aisle without him.

I keep my eyes on the cash register ahead of me, seeing behind the counter and through the wall behind it. Only blackness lingers between the trees; it's a creepy sight. This reminds me why I choose to reside in cities where there are streetlamps and people just about everywhere.

My heart nearly stops when Finn appears right in front of me. I slap a hand over my chest. "You scared me."

"Stay with me," he commands.

"Okay." Considering how hard my heart is pounding, that sounds like the best option.

"Look," he says, pointing toward the cement floor.

I follow his finger through the ground and into a tiny chamber where a heavyset man with a full beard sits on a cot. He's so still that if his eyes weren't blinking, I'd think he was dead.

"Is he still human?" I ask.

"Get a good look at him and take a sniff," Finn tells me.

I hesitate as he sets those hypnotizing eyes on my face. Then I do as I'm told.

"Smell that?" he asks.

At first, I smell nothing, but then I go deeper. I see past his skin and into his body. Dear God, there's his heart, lungs, and all sorts of vessels and organs working together to keep him alive.

"He smells like burning coal," I finally say.

"That's how humans smell when they're alive. When they're dead, they smell like rot."

"What do I smell like?" I ask.

"Lime and mint." He walks off. "Taste like it too."

I snort as I follow him. I would've never guessed that. But I have no time to muse about the aroma of *me*. As we progress toward the register, the open space behind me holds a threatening energy.

Before I know it, Finn's face is right in front of mine. He cups my chin. "If you're afraid, don't show me."

I feel my entire face frown. I wonder why he would say such a thing until I read the vulnerability in his eyes. I kind of, sort of understand. On top of everything else, he shouldn't have to worry about *me*. He can't have a partner who's an incessant damsel in distress. Especially if he could "love" her.

"Okay," I say. "But I'm not scared; I'm cautious."

Finn nods. "I'll take that."

He spins around on his heels and leaps over the counter with ease. I do the same. Once I land on my feet, I take a moment to soak in what I just did. That was so easy! My body feels as though it could've flown over the barrier if I'd wanted it to. Maybe that's adrenaline.

"Down here," Finn says. He squats and presses his hand against the dusty floor.

We're right above the cot and the bearded man. The guy knows we're here too. He's staring at the ceiling, his face red and his blue eyes filled with horror.

"How do we get down there?" I ask.

The floor crumbles, and Finn throws his arms around me as we fall into the dark chamber. There's no impact at all when our feet hit the ground. Finn studies my face to see if I'm okay before he lets go of me. When we turn toward the human, he's pointing a rifle at Finn's head. *Does everyone in this town own a shotgun?*

Finn wastes no time turning the man's weapon into dust.

"What do you want with me?" the man cries while scooting back on the cot. His back smashes into the wall.

"Why are you down here?" Finn asks as he steps toward him.

The man throws his arms up to block his face. "Who are you?"

This guy is very afraid. I'm on the verge of

telling him we're here to help when Finn wraps his hand around the man's stocky neck.

"What are *you* doing down here?" Finn demands.

The guy is gasping for air.

"Finn!" My pulse is racing because I'm sure he's either going to choke him or break his neck.

Finn twists around to look at me. I'm caught off guard by the look in his eyes. There's no anger, or frustration, or even hate. He looks as if he's done this a million times, and this is just part of the procedure.

"You're going to kill him," I say feebly, amazed by his eerie calm.

Finn narrows his eyes at me before letting go of the guy's neck. The stout man rolls off the cot and collapses, coughing and holding his neck. Finn studies him, waiting for him to regroup.

After a moment, I rush over to kneel beside the man. "Are you okay?"

"Stay the hell away from me," the guy cries while scooting in the opposite direction.

"I'm not going to hurt you," I assure him. "All we want to know is why you were left down here. There has to be a reason, because just about everyone else in town is missing."

"I wasn't left anywhere," he says.

"Are you hiding?"

His eyes shift between Finn and me. "Who the hell are you?"

When I look at Finn, he's sniffing the air. The guy and I watch Finn as he kneels to scoop up a handful of dust from the floor he just destroyed.

"It's silver," Finn says, narrowing his eyes at the guy.

"How can you touch it?" the man asks, shocked.

Finn just scowls at him. From experience, I know he's not going to answer.

"Is that why you're down here? Because the silver protects you from vampires?" I ask.

"Yeah," the guy says while nodding. "I came here to hide when they broke into the store and started carting people off—" He stops short.

I suspect he was going to say something else but chose not to reveal something. I know he still doesn't trust us. "Listen. We're not with *those guys*."

He looks at Finn. "What about him?"

Finn just peers at the guy with his trademark scowl.

"No. He's with me."

"I know a vampire when I see one," he says.

Finn doesn't react.

"I've already grasped that part. But what about me?" I ask.

He narrows his eyes to examine me. "Are you here to do his bidding?"

"No, but you sound pretty aware of things only crazy people are supposed to believe in. So yes, Finn is a vampire. I'm Glo, and I'm not. We're trying to figure out what's going on here in your town."

"They want to turn us all into *them*," the guy declares. He sounds pretty sure about it. He has the same deep southern drawl as Suzanne.

"That's what *we* suspect too," I say.

The guy seems to relax. "I've been doing the watching." He pauses, as if his words threatened to get away from him. "When I can, at least..." He pushes himself to his feet, although he's making an effort to keep as far away from Finn as possible. "They haven't turned them all yet, but they want to."

I feel hopeful all of a sudden. "So there are still some people left?"

He gives Finn the once-over and says, "This way."

As he steps away, I follow, but we both stop in awe as all the particles from the disintegrated floor flow upward. The ceiling is perfectly reassembled, as if the floor never gave way.

"Finn, did you do that?" My eyes are still wide with amazement.

"Yes," he replies.

"I didn't know you could put things back together again."

"Now you do."

I think he's smiling at me with his eyes, but I'm not sure. He's still a hard one to read.

"By the way," the guy says, seeming impressed by Finn's latest stunt, "my name is Obadiah." He holds his hand out for me to shake it.

"Nice to meet you, Obadiah." I'm glad to finally earn a kernel of his trust.

"Naw, just call me Ob."

"Then nice to meet you, Ob."

He hesitates then holds a jittery hand out for Finn to shake. Finn narrows his eyes as if he's contemplating whether or not he should touch Ob. I want to assure Finn that Ob won't give him the cooties, but Finn reaches out to give him a weak handshake.

"You're warm," Ob says, sounding surprised.

"You've touched a vampire before?" Finn asks suspiciously.

A veil of sadness falls over his eyes. "My son had some dealings with them. This way."

We follow Obadiah through a door and down a long, dark corridor. Although he seems nice, my instincts advise me to remain cautious. From the way Finn observes our surroundings, I gather his are telling him the same thing.

"I built these caverns," Obadiah boasts, guiding us through the dimness.

"What about him?" Finn says as he appears in front of Obadiah. He's holding up the photo of Suzanne's husband. "Did he help you?"

"Dell?" Obadiah says as if the wind's been knocked out of him. "Who gave you that?"

"His wife," Finn says. "She said she hid in a panic room. I saw it. It's made of silver."

My face drops. I'm disappointed he didn't share that detail with me. Could Suzanne have already known about the existence of vampires? Did Finn already realize that about her?

"They didn't get her?"

"Apparently not," Finn says. "But you're foolish to think you can fight vampires with silver bullets and guns."

Obadiah lets out a sarcastic grunt. "Well, I

know that now. The only thing we got right was these containment structures."

"You think?" Finn is being sarcastic too, but I'm not sure Obadiah gets it.

"Wait," I say. "Suzanne had silver bullets in her rifles?"

"Yes," Finn says.

Obadiah watches as I glare at Finn, who looks perplexed. He evidently has no idea why I'm upset. I let out a cleansing sigh and shake my head. Why am I wasting energy being angry? He doesn't have the capacity to understand that I feel left out, especially because he's always done this sort of thing alone.

I shift my eyes back to Obadiah and nod a little to the right. "Are we going in there?"

He hesitates. I'm sure he's wondering how I saw the small room.

"Yes," he mutters.

"Then lead on." My annoyance with Finn bleeds into my tone.

In the middle of the tight chamber is an island with a bunch of old, bulky televisions lined up on it. The screens on all five monitors are black, but one of them is clearly turned on.

Obadiah rushes over and turns knobs on the off

ones. "They must've cut the power, but why is this one still on?" He's panicking a little.

"Do you see what's there?" Finn asks me, staring into the one working screen. He's purposely ignoring Obadiah's minor breakdown.

I study the black screen. At first all I see is a dark empty space. I use my second sight to see within the darkness and I gasp when my eyes come across a plastic box like the kind the chemist handed Cort. It's sitting on a table that's pushed up against the wall. The box is nearly empty. It only contains about twenty white pills. I look at Finn, and he meets my eyes.

"*Zombies,*" he telepathically says.

Obadiah notices us staring into the monitor. "That right there is up under the Shack. Every now and then, the door opens, and I can see inside. Only at night though. That's when they come." He doesn't realize that Finn and I are having an entirely different conversation just between the two of us.

"*Look past this room,*" Finn tells me.

I do as I'm told. There's a wide open, dimly lit space with a whole lot of people in cages. They seem to be divided in groups: kids, women, and men. They look miserable, exhausted, and traumatized at the same time. Some of the younger children are simply whimpering. Their faces are soaking wet; they've been crying for a very long time and are running out of steam. A sweet woman's voice is singing "Hush Little Baby." Even the adults' eyes are closed as they allow themselves to be soothed.

"We have to get those people out of there!" I shout in his head. I mean *now*. I look at Finn with desperation.

Finn stands firm and calmly declares, *"No. We should wait."*

"Wait?" I shout.

Obadiah stiffens; he's obviously confused, thinking that I just told him to wait. I'm in a frenzy. I'm panting and looking around as if I can't get out of this cold cave fast enough. I'm ready to run off and turn every vampire who tries to get in my way into ashes. For the first time since Finn and I started out together, I'm ready to *slay*.

"Wait for what?" Obadiah's eyes shuffle back and forth between Finn and me.

"I know you don't care about people, but—" I say out loud.

"I don't?" Finn asks. "I've been saving humans since way before you were born."

"That's not what you said. You said they were disposable."

"I said I don't involve humans in vampire affairs, not that they were disposable," he retorts.

I blink. I truly need to steady myself. Finn is not the enemy, and a hot head is cluttered with smoke. In our dangerous situation, my head has to stay clear and sharp.

"Where do you see humans?" Obadiah asks, searching the screens.

"They're there," I say, still staring at Finn. "You just can't see them."

"And you can?"

"If you care about those humans, then you'll have patience," Finn says, once again ignoring Obadiah. *"They know I'm here, and they're waiting for me. Look farther."*

I tear my eyes from his face and see past the horrendous sight of people caged up like animals. He's right. Vampires are posted around the walls outside the prison. Each one of them has a finger on the lever of a high-intensity blowtorch.

"Are they looking to burn you alive?" I ask, appalled by the fact that someone wants to kill *him*. I'm embarrassed to admit even to myself that I think of him as *my Finn*.

His expression goes from blank to that perplexed look he always has. It only lasts a few seconds. He hands me the photo of Suzanne's husband. *"Do you see him anywhere?"*

I check the image of the thin, ginger-haired man who's sneering at the camera. He's wearing a mustard-colored T-shirt and is standing in what looks like a backyard, over a grill, waving a spatula. He's an everyday person, for goodness sake! How is this happening to people like him?

I search through the cages of contained people. As I go from one despondent face to the next, my stomach, which never turns, turns.

Obadiah wiggles a finger between Finn and me. "Wait, are you two talking to each other without speaking?"

Finn lifts a strong hand at him, gesturing for him to remain silent. At first Ob flinches, but something makes him nod and keep quiet. That's funny, because Ob doesn't strike me as the obedient sort of guy. I've gathered that he likes to be in control of a situation.

"I know you want to save the humans," Finn says to regain my attention. *"I love that about you. But I have a job to do, and there's only one thing I need."*

"Cort." I know that's why he's being careful not

to create too much of a ruckus. He doesn't want to scare off the fox.

Finn lifts his eyebrows, confirming my conclusion.

"You lost him because of me, didn't you?" I ask.

"Yes," he says.

"Did he suspect it was you who orchestrated the burning incident at the lab?"

"He knows I collapsed the tunnels. He thinks a Sham helped me with a burning curse. Tal went off to find out who that is. Now he's trying to throw me off his trail before he comes back to finish up here."

"Why does he want to change these people into vampires?" I ask.

"Cort isn't working on his own behalf. He's working for an evil son-of-a-bitch named Exgesis. Exgesis is the father of second-generation vampires like Cort."

"The ones who can drink other vampires."

"Right. Exgesis is delusional. He thinks if he changes humankind into vampires, then he'll be the new God."

"That sounds maniacal."

"It is."

"And Cort and Exgesis let you hear all of this? Or do they know you can see and hear them?"

"They don't know what I look like. Not many other vampires on Earth do. The same should go for you. Are you

ready for another lesson in humanity?" Finn asks me while glaring at Obadiah.

"*What lesson?*" I ask.

Suddenly Finn has Obadiah by the neck *again*. Obadiah struggles to retain consciousness. Words want to break past my lips, but I'm still in shock.

"If I let you go," Finn growls, his mouth close to Obadiah's ear, "I want you to start telling us the truth. Deal?"

Finn lets up enough so that Obadiah can nod. Accepting his gesture, Finn lets go, and Obadiah slumps to the ground, coughing.

"Why did you do that?" I finally ask as I step toward Obadiah.

This time, Finn puts an arm out to stop me. In his eyes, Obadiah is dangerous. "The truth." Finn glares at the man he almost choked to death.

Obadiah coughs. "I had to help them."

"*Help* them?" I'm terribly confused.

"They have my son."

I must look incredulous because Finn says, "The wiring on the cameras to the monitors goes two ways."

"So what you're saying is"—I point at the only monitor that's on—"we can see them and they can see us."

"I destroyed the lines to all the other cameras and monitors before we entered the room. That's why the vampires are guarding the prisons. They know my work."

Ob says, "They said they were going to kill my son if I didn't find a way to get them what they wanted. I had to do it."

"And what did they want?" I ask.

He sighs. There's a lot of remorse in his expression. "They wanted the people here. Dell agreed to help me. We were trying to find a way around it. But…"

"Your son, is he still human?" Finn asks.

Obadiah clutches his chest and drops and shakes his head. "I don't know what the hell's going on anymore. I figured I'd just do it and get my boy back in whatever state he's in."

The entire circumstance everyone in this town has found themselves in is unreal. I can't imagine going back to life as usual after this. Their souls have aged. So has mine.

Finn aims a finger at the monitor that's on. "Have you seen who's been going in and out that room?"

"Well, yeah, that's where we talk. I ain't ever seen them in person, only there."

"Them?"

"One with long white hair, strange-looking fella, and—"

"Exgesis," Finn growls.

I've never seen so much hate in his crystal-clear eyes. There's something else too. A change. A flicker of realizing impending doom, possibly.

"All right," Finn says to me. "You're about to get what you want." He turns to Obadiah. "Your silver doesn't work on a vampire like Exgesis. Your best bet is to stay away from him and his cronies because when he's done *using* you, he will kill you. Where's Suzanne's husband?"

Obadiah drops his face again, and his shoulders shake because he's crying. I'm stunned. In all of my life, I've never heard a man cry. It's the saddest thing in the world.

He moans "Larry" over and over again.

"We can help you get your son back," I say, although I'm not really sure we can. I look to Finn. "Can't we?"

"Maybe," Finn answers, which is a relief. I've been around him long enough to know that he'd never answer in the affirmative if there wasn't a strong possibility of a favorable outcome. But then he says, "Maybe not."

CHAPTER 8
THE REVEAL

After Finn worked his magic and repaired the lines to the cameras and monitors he'd earlier destroyed, he instructed Obadiah to continue monitoring as if nothing had changed. At the crack of dawn, he's to get out of the caves, into sunlight, and down to the B&B. That's where he's to stay. From this point on, he'll have to rely on Finn and me.

"Do you think he'll do what you said?" I ask Finn as we move through a dark tunnel made of a huge, rusted metal drum that's buried about twenty feet in the earth. This is such an elaborate set-up that it's impossible to believe all of this was done without at least half of the town knowing about it.

"If he knows what's best for him," Finn answers.

"Hey, Finn?" I wait for him to look at me. I want to see his face when I ask this next question.

He faces me.

"You figured it all out before we even walked into the room, didn't you?" I ask.

"Yes."

"You didn't trust Obadiah from the beginning, did you?"

"He can't be trusted."

"Why not?"

"He has one goal, and that's to get his son back. That makes him single-minded."

He's studying me with that dubious expression again, but I stare straight ahead. That's when I see that we don't have too far to go before we run into an actual brick wall. I'm training my instincts to see past all primary barriers at first sight. That's where Finn has the advantage; he's already proficient in doing this.

"Are you afraid?" That's what he's searching my face for now: fear.

I shake my head. "No."

"Are you confused or…"

I crack a tiny smirk. "I'm always confused when it comes to you."

"You find *me* confusing," he mutters. That wasn't a question.

As we stand at the wall facing each other, he *is* fully affecting me. He says I smell like mint and lime, but so does he. Our faces are so close. I want him to kiss me again, but then I look upward. This isn't the appropriate place to make out with Finn the sexy vampire.

"They're up there," I whisper, restraining my desires.

First, I see Finn disappear before my eyes. Next, I hear loud thuds, grunts, and growls. Then a huge guy wearing slacks, shoes, and a black coat is standing over Finn. He's watching me with blue eyes that glow, and his palm is aimed at Finn. A blue energy flows out of it and pins Finn to the metal floor. Finn grunts as he struggles against the force to no avail.

"I'm Echo Leon," the man says. He's calm, and his talking voice sounds like a roar. He's not the least bit concerned about Finn freeing himself from his power.

"Aries mentioned you. You're a guardian," I say

as my eyes shift between Finn and the blue-eyed angel.

"The Guardian to the fifth daughter of the House of Benel."

"Yes." I'm still caught off guard by how formal he sounds, as if he's making a royal proclamation. I bob my head while staring at Finn, who has stopped struggling although he clearly hates being overwhelmed. "Could you let him go?"

Without a word of debate, Echo Leon releases the force, and Finn is free. Finn goes for the attack. This time, Echo Leon tosses him, and Finn crashes into the metal wall.

"Finn, stop!" I yell before he attacks again.

To my surprise, he does.

"This is Echo Leon, my Guardian," I say to Finn. By the way Echo Leon glances at me and then at Finn, I suspect he heard me.

"A Guardian?" Finn grunts at Echo Leon.

"Aries said I'll meet him. I guess now's the time."

"Is he an angel?" Finn asks me.

"I am not an angel," Echo Leon says, confirming my suspicion. He *can* hear us.

If he isn't an angel, he sure looks like one. His blue eyes are stunning against his golden skin, and they haven't stopped glowing. He's also clutching what looks to be a sword covered with blue flames. He has no hair, not even eyebrows, and his features are as sharp as if they've been carved out of stone. He's truly a work of art.

"We have thirty-seven minutes before sunrise," Echo Leon says as he looks up.

I'm positive he sees what we see. He rests his eyes on me. I'm waiting for him to say something else, but he doesn't. He stands there like a soldier, waiting for the next order.

Right now, about fifty creatures that were once human but are now vampires stand along the walls outside the holding chamber directly above us. Also, a number of them are sitting at tables in the main bar, knocking back glasses of whatever liquor is still left in the place. Yes, they're vampires, but I would rather not harm them. However, we seem to have no choice. It's a hard reality, so I prepare myself to face it.

"I guess now's the time," I say to Finn.

He's busy frowning at Echo Leon. I don't think Finn hears how shaky my voice is or senses how nervous I am. He just looks as though wants the other guy gone.

"Finn," I call to get his attention.

He flicks his eyes over to me.

"You need to"—I point my thumb up at the ceiling—"make a way in." And in a hurry. I'm losing all of my nerve.

After giving us the Finn face one more time, he turns to me, looks up, and says, "I need you to steady the earth around the opening. The soil's too wet; it won't hold for long."

I remember my exercise with the trees and their leaves. Instead of shifting the soil as I did the leaves, I think of the soil separating the top of the round drum from the base of the Shack as a block of unmovable cement.

"I've done it," I say, sounding surprised that it worked but sure of myself at the same time.

Finn must trust me because the next thing I know, a gully about fifteen feet wide and twenty-five feet deep has been blown out above us. I can see the ceiling of the basement where the townspeople are being held captive. The cut has been carved with the precision of a surgeon's scalpel. There's still a good five feet between the cages and the hole, to prevent people from falling in. Finn's mind is always two or three steps ahead.

"How will I get up there?" I mutter while watching the younger children cry harder. Even the adults wail, pray, and tremble with fear.

"You'll ride the wind," Echo Leon says at the same time Finn says, "I'll carry you."

Both Finn and I ask, "Ride the wind?"

"Yes, you let yourself walk on air. You just do it because you can. Are you ready?" Echo Leon asks me.

Anxiety chokes every nerve in my body. I can walk on air? I have no time to doubt myself because all the crying is putting the vampires guarding the prison on edge.

I look at Finn. "Are we ready?"

Finn appears disturbed by the fact that Echo Leon isn't behaving as if he knows who's really in charge here. However, Finn knows there's no time to engage in a power struggle. One of the vampires patrolling the hallways has already opened the door. Finn just nods while glaring daggers at Echo Leon, who has no reaction to the dirty look.

The blue-eyed guardian turns to me and orders me, "Go!"

He says it so loudly and forcefully that I don't take a moment to doubt myself. I tell myself to walk on air, and lo and behold, my feet are off the ground! Not only am I rising, but I'm moving pretty quickly. Finn is right beside me. We study each other but only for a brief second. The vampires

221

have come into the room, and about six of them are standing over the opening. They watch us with deep curiosity, but that only lasts a fraction of a second before they aim their blowtorches at us. Finn turns their weapons into dust.

We almost make it to the top before the vampires choose option two: leaping over the edge. They're coming at us. Six on three. Two for me. Two for Finn. Two for Echo Leon.

A huge lump of anticipation is caught in my throat. The two coming at me have their glazed eyes narrowed to slits, and they're snarling.

They have one goal: kill me.

If they can.

Because something inside me clicks. What I do next is not only about kill or be killed—it's about stop and save. I visualize bubbly molten lava racing down an active volcano. I visualize the lava drenching the two vampires who are only a few feet away from me.

The effect is immediate. Flames engulf them. They swat and try to kick away the fire that burns off their clothes and coats their skin. I can hardly stand to hear them crying. It's almost too much for me to bear. Then a heap of ashes barely misses me. I look up as Echo Leon's sword slices through another vampire, and she bursts into ashes too. This time I dart over to the wall and press my back against the damp earth to avoid being drenched by vampire debris.

I didn't see what happened to the two who had attacked Finn. He's already out of the fissure and walking in front of the cages with a finger pressed to his lips, telling the people to remain quiet. It's only working with the adults though. Some of them call across to the very little children, who are clinging to the bars and wailing. They try to soothe and quiet them as much as the chaos around them will allow. However, they might as well have saved their breath. Once Echo Leon and I reach the floor, more vampires file into the room, and the children cry so hard that a few of them pass out.

Finn walks toward the new vampires, pulverizing them into tiny pieces with his eyes. They become a heap of mush. Echo Leon's sword slices and dices. He's too fast for them to lay their hands on him, but it doesn't stop them from trying.

I'm flustered, twisting and turning and stinging my aggressors with lava heat before they can get to me. It's only when I feel two prongs against my jugular that I realize how close they're actually getting. The pressure of the canine teeth disappears as the owner turns to ashes. All I see now is a blue blade slicing around me, turning what were once living beings into debris.

Screams, moans, cries, growls, grunts, and expletives ring out. I'm more in control now that Echo Leon has helped me out of a tight spot. The aggressors are dwindling in numbers but not in resolve. Two of them aim blowtorches at me. As the fire comes out, I throw my arms up to instinctively shield myself, and the fire hits an invisible barrier. My mind has created an actual shield! The flames hit it until their weapons disintegrate. Then they become jelly themselves.

Now I can decipher all of our handiwork. I leave behind charred corpses. Echo Leon turns them into black ashes. Finn turns them into mush.

I'm standing firm, eyes on alert, still holding my shield around me. Drops of ice pelt my skin, and I look up. There's no roof on this place. The sun breaks in the sky. The walls that form the upper structure dissolve into a substance as fine as baby powder. Next the bars on the cages that contain the townspeople dissolve, and the fissure in the ground closes.

As the cold hits me, I notice I'm the only one of the three of us left. Echo Leon is gone, and so is

Finn. I twist around, searching for them, but all I see are the parents scooping up their children. People are hugging, crying, and asking each other if they're okay.

"You," a woman says to me. She's so pale, except around her eyes; the skin there is so purple that it looks as though she has two black eyes. "Thank you!"

In slow motion, I watch her step toward me and throw her arms around me. She clings to me, and all I want to do is cry with her. This is a horrible experience to live through. The children are shaking and clinging to their parents. I might as well be invisible to these people who are rediscovering their freedom.

"Tell them to go home, lock the doors, and don't let anyone in," Finn says to me.

That's exactly what I tell the woman. I shout Finn's instructions loud enough for everyone else to hear me. I shout them over and over until I watch flustered people, who are still sort of confused about what to do next, rush down the icy road and branch off in different directions.

I'm shivering and wet when Finn says, *"Please get inside the truck."*

I turn to my left, and there's our black vehicle

parked alongside the road in front of where the Shack used to stand. I run to where it's warm and dry. Once I slide into the truck and shut the door, Finn takes one of my hands and touches my neck.

"You're bleeding," he says, holding up two fingers stained with blood.

I see the way his eyes gleam at the blood on his fingers and my neck. He swallows hard. I think he wants to taste it, but instead, he sniffs it. Then he puts the two bloody fingers close to my nose.

"Smell," he says.

I inhale deeply. Finn was right—my blood does smell like mint and lime.

"That's why you were bitten. At least one of them smelled you. There's a power in your blood," he says while he stares into my face. Finn then rubs his bloody fingers together.

I watch my blood flake away as powder. *How does he do that?* I turn to watch the Shack re-erect itself. "Wow! I'm always impressed when you do that."

"You're wet," Finn says.

I turn to face him. He's looking at me in that way again. It's the way his eyes ravished me before he made love to me only yesterday. At the moment, I feel as though that happened years ago.

"Yeah." I turn away from him. Just him mentioning it reminds me of how uncomfortable I am in my damp clothes.

He starts the truck and drives. "I'll take you to the B&B so you can get dry and cleaned up."

Sounds like a great idea. I definitely need warm water to wash away the remains of the terrible battle. "What about you?"

"I'll keep an eye out for whoever comes. I'm hoping it's Exgesis. I'd like to kill him and get it over with," he says, muttering the last part.

I can tell by the way he's gripping the steering wheel and how he's pulled his mouth tight that he means it.

It's a relief to see that Obadiah made the right decision and got to the B&B at the crack of dawn just like Finn told him to. I had my doubts, and I think Finn did too because he's already allowed desperation to lead him to a very dark place. However, I had seen a spark of realization in Ob's eyes when Finn warned him about that Exgesis vampire. I think Obadiah had suspected a double cross all along.

The way the diner smells in the morning fills the downstairs of the B&B. It's the aroma of coffee, bacon, pancakes, and maple syrup. The scent used to make my mouth water, but now it makes my stomach turn, and I gag. Strangely enough, I'm craving fruit.

I nearly drop my bag when I see Suzanne's husband Dell, whom I recognize from the photograph, standing beside her. I can't help but wonder where he's been all this time. Unlike the others, his face isn't gaunt. He doesn't look hungry, exhausted, or traumatized. Heck, even I look more worn than he does. Something definitely isn't right, but I've learned from Finn to keep my suspicions to myself.

"Where have you been all of this time?" I ask him, because it's the next logical question. I make sure to keep my eyes soft.

He hesitates before saying, "I've been working with Ob, trying to catch these characters. You know, the vampires."

"Yeah," I say with a sigh. "Well, I'm going to get cleaned up." I start up the stairs to find an empty room.

"What happened out there?" Obadiah asks.

I almost forgot he's in the room. He's not too far away from Dell—they're acutely aware of each other's presence. Whatever they're *in*, in their minds, they're still in it together. I turn my head to see the gas station and into the cellar where the monitors are. According to the monitors, nothing's changed; the empty room with the Zombies in it is still dark and empty.

"Just stay out of the Shack," I say. "Finn's keeping an eye on it, making sure nobody goes in or out."

"He left you here by yourself?" Dell asks.

What a strange question. "Why? Is it dangerous in here?" I ask.

Dell's eyes widen with exaggerated concern. "My wife told me you and your partner said this place is safe. It seems to be. You're just so beaten up. Will you be all right up there by yourself?"

I narrow my eyes at Dell. He's not to be trusted; his very essence is duplicitous. I have a feeling he's the one who set up the cameras and the underground tunnels and helped round up all the people of this town and put them in dark prisons. I want to end him here and now, but I have to do what Finn would do—watch him like a hawk and expect a double cross.

I sigh tiredly. "I'll be fine, but thanks for your concern."

"I made breakfast," Suzanne says, offering me a seat at the table.

"Thank you, but I'm not hungry," I reply without looking back or stopping on my way up the stairs.

I can't believe how angry I am at Dell and Obadiah, but I control it as I finish mounting the stairs, keeping my steps soft. After peering through all of the rooms, I find a large empty one with a bathroom at the end of the hall. I go there fast, taking advantage of the superhuman speed I discovered I have. As I strip out of my wet pants, coat, and sweater, I keep my eyes and ears on the people downstairs.

"I know the vampire can," Ob whispers. "Not sure about the girl."

"I don't think she can do much," Dell says, quite sure of himself.

"Come to think of it, I don't think so either." Obadiah rubs his neck, reminiscing. "He's been doing all the heavy lifting. But they can talk to each other without saying anything. That's something."

"That ain't nothing, Ob," Dell exclaims. "Hell, so can me and Suzie!"

Suzanne drops a plate of food in front of him.

She's upset, and when Dell reaches out to touch her, she shrugs away from him.

"You could've told me something," she barks at him, failing to keep her voice down. "And that girl helped us."

"I was looking out for you, Suzie," he says in his defense.

"We were scared, Dell! Your children thought you were dead!"

Dell glances over his shoulder to see if the coast is still clear. "Quiet down."

"Why?" she asks, setting her chin in defiance. "Why did you do this to our neighbors, to our friends, to our kids?"

That's a good question. I'm caught between wrapping myself in a towel and twisting my long locks into a bun as I pause to hear the answer.

"Not now," Dell growls between clenched teeth. He looks so ominous that she flinches.

Suzanne takes a deep breath and mutters, "I'm going to get the kids." She rushes out of the room with teary eyes.

I never realized until now that Dell must have some motive in helping Obadiah recover his son. I mean, imprisoning the entire town to help a friend without getting something for his trouble is too far-fetched. He had to bury metal drums and obtain enough silver to spread it across the ceiling and walls of the small chamber Obadiah sought refuge in. None of what they've done is free; obtaining that amount of silver would cost a pretty penny! Dell has to have done all this to get something. The only thing I can think of is what I know inspires a lot of people to do evil: money.

I shower fast, scrubbing the remains of the early morning off my skin and shampooing it out of my hair. Although the warm water makes me want to close my eyes and relax, I keep them open and on the men downstairs. The two children have joined Dell and Obadiah at the table. There's a lot of tension in the air, but no one's saying a word. I'm waiting for one of the men to head upstairs to try to confront me. I'm not sure how I'll handle it. Then I remember Finn is always watching.

Finn is always watching.

As I stand in the shower, I look past the kitchen and across the weather-beaten lawn to the front seat of the truck. We make eye contact, Finn and I. He's staring at me, and shamelessly at that. The crazy part is that I don't want him to look away. Instead of covering myself, I just face him, inviting him to me.

"We've got fog, and Obadiah is on the move. Get dressed and get out of there. Make sure you're not seen," he says.

Without taking his eyes off my body, he saw Obadiah creep out the back door. *Man, he's good.*

It's foggy outside, and it's getting thicker by the second. We both watch Ob haul his heavy body across the manicured backyard until he reaches a woody plot of land with a hatch in the ground. He lifts the hatch and enters head first, crawling down one of those metal drums. He reaches another cylinder of the same kind, and it leads right to the gas station.

Dell is heading up the stairs with his hand in his pocket, clutching a sharp carving knife. I think he's planning on using it on me. I waste no time slipping on fresh underwear, a dry pair of jeans, and a sweater. I use my eyes to dry my boots, as I used to do in college when my shoes got drenched from walking from class to the dorm in bad weather.

After I slip on my boots and grab my bag, I hurry to the bay doors that lead to the balcony. I move fast, getting outside, swerving around a garden table, and leaping over the ledge. I land steadily on my feet. As I look up into the bedroom, I see that Dell is skulking around it; he thinks I'm still in the bathroom. It's only when I get in the truck and Finn drives off that Dell realizes I'm not there.

"Guess who rolled in with the fog?" Finn asks, still looking at me as if I'm naked.

"Cort?"

"Better. It's two birds: Exgesis and Cort."

I swallow hard and nod. It's difficult for me to stay focused when he looks at me like that. He has power over me. Of this I'm sure.

"Is that where Obadiah's gone?" I ask.

"Take a look in his old cave," Finn says as the truck stops in front of the Shack.

He forces his eyes off me to look way across the small town at the gas station, which is a little over a mile away. Cort is facing Obadiah, who just walked into the room we first found him in. I look away and see a tall, thin, red-haired guy trotting down the road toward us. Although he's wrapped in a thick winter coat with the hood covering most of his face, I can see that it's Dell. He keeps checking over his shoulders, hoping not to be seen as he rushes past Finn's invisible truck.

He uses a key to unlock the door of the Shack, and he slips inside. We watch him speed walk across the parquet floors and into the kitchen. He opens the doors to what looks like a pantry and squats down. He pulls a tiny lever, and the wall slides open.

"Wow, these guys leave no stones unturned," I whisper.

Finn remains silent, so instinctively I turn to see if his face shows any reaction to my comment. To my surprise, he's staring at me with fire in his eyes. He quickly pulls me into him, and with his arms around me, he continues watching the scene unfold.

I, on the other hand, can hardly breathe, let alone concentrate. Finn's much more relaxed than I am. I don't want him to let me go, so I coach myself into getting a grip. His chest is so hard, yet soft and warm. My body feels as if it just clicked its heels three times and has found its way home. When I finally put my eyes back on Dell, he's in that small dark room where the few Zombies are being stored.

"Where in the hell are my humans?" the white-haired guy shouts, working himself into an all-out frenzy. He's a weird-looking individual. His hair is all white, but his skin is a rich tan. He reminds me of someone. Not a real person—a cartoon character.

"Yes," I say once I realize who he resembles. "He looks like the evil prince Lotor in the *Voltron* cartoons. Don't you think? Except his hair isn't gray and his skin isn't blue." I marvel at the sight of this Exgesis character. He's definitely something to behold.

"Why are you looking at Exgesis that way?" Finn asks, disrupting my ogling.

"I've just never seen anyone who looks like that before."

Finn loosens his grip on me. "You're really into the male, aren't you?"

I frown hard, confused. "You mean like a man?"

"The human, Upton. You were really into him."

"Okay, that's one."

"Me? You're into me."

"Who said I was into you?"

"You wouldn't let me do what I did to you if you weren't into me."

"And what did I let you do to me?"

He tilts his head and gives me a look that says *you know what I'm referring to*.

I sigh and shrug, deciding to stop pretending. We're not children, for goodness sake. "Okay. Yes, I'm into you. I've been into you since I first saw you."

I've been watching Finn during our entire conversation, but he hasn't taken his eyes off of

Exgesis and Dell. I'll let him do the watching. At the moment, I'm more concerned with his reaction to what I just said.

There's no frown on his face when he says, "Me too."

I feel my heart take a dive and splash into fountains of joy. I mean, yes, Exgesis is interesting, but only in the same way that a butterfly with the body of a praying mantis would be. Finn… Well, he's the embodiment of heaven. He's the lush green garden that's cool in the day under the showers of peace. Finn is my forever; that I'm sure of.

This time, I press my lips to his. Gently, slowly, deeply, he kisses me back. Now that I've identified that luscious scent of his, I can taste it on his tongue and lips.

"You should look at what's happening," he whispers between kisses.

"I know," I say. This is the worst time to be doing this, but I couldn't resist. My head is still spinning, and I feel loopy, but I go back to watching the man and the vampire.

"I'm simply not happy with the situation we're in," Exgesis says, feigning self-control. He could obviously blow at any second.

"We can get them back," Dell assures him.

Exgesis laughs out loud. It's the most sinister sound I've ever heard.

"You don't know what happened here, do you?" he spits.

Dell frowns at him, confused.

Exgesis looks up at a pen-sized camera in the corner of the ceiling. "Go ahead, Cort. Show the slayer what I just revealed to you. I know he's watching."

I glance at Finn, who has his arms wrapped tightly around me again. He's snarling at Exgesis. I fear that at any minute, he'll disappear from the truck and go kill Exgesis with his bare hands. My eyes shift to the gas station cellar where Obadiah stands next to Cort. Without warning, Cort grabs Ob. The next thing I know, his teeth are in Ob's neck. Obadiah is yelling, crying out for him to stop.

I'm caught in a moment of shock. I believed that vampires couldn't drink from a human without permission. When my shock passes, I conjure a hot shield that coats Obadiah's body. Right away, Cort yells and holds his mouth. He rolls on the floor in pain, and his mouth is smoking. Obadiah has passed out.

"Don't do anything else," Finn scolds me as he releases me.

The truck engine cuts on. I watch Cort flow into one of the cylinders that leads to the room where Exgesis is standing.

"That was just a sample, Finn the vin, nin, zin," Exgesis sings mockingly. He turns in circles, knowing the vampire slayer is watching. "That's one down." He points upward and to the east. "One to go."

I sense that he's pointing to something in particular, so I follow where his finger leads. "The sun!"

Exgesis turns his sinister grin onto Dell, who hasn't taken his eyes off of Cort's bloody lips. "Good thing for you I prefer vampire blood."

I notice Exgesis's general way of speaking sounds taunting. Where others would have to work at it, he doesn't. With one glance at Finn, I see how much he hates this vampire. There's got to be more to it than just fighting an evil vampire. They must have history.

To my surprise, Finn grits his teeth and mutters, "Do it, Glo. Light them up."

I waste no time coating Exgesis in my mental lava, and I don't forget about Cort either. Cort goes up in flames, yelling as he becomes charcoal right before our eyes. But Exgesis only has a little smoke rising from his skin.

I intensify the heat. Cort goes along as I conjure up a flaming pit to drop both lava-covered vampires in. Cort turns into a lump of coal, and my heart sinks, hating that I killed him so easily. I mean, who made us judge, jury, and executioner? Although more smoke comes off of Exgesis's skin, there are no flames.

"He's being protected," Finn mumbles with a snarl.

Then Finn is out of the truck, and Exgesis is out of the room. Finn is in the room, and he's in trouble.

CHAPTER 9

A DRINK OF NECTAR

We're in a serious pickle. Just that brief time in the sun has Finn's skin smoking like a chimney. He's in that dark room in the Shack, bent over, gritting his teeth, and grunting in pain. I need to get him back to the truck, but I can't unless I take the truck to him.

Dell fumbles the carving knife out of his pants pocket and runs at Finn with it. Before Finn can react, I heat up the entire instrument. The plastic handle melts in Dell's hand. He drops it and grabs his limb, wailing in agony as the substance bubbles on his skin.

I scoot to the driver's seat, intending to drive right through the front door of the Shack, but Finn appears beside me in the passenger seat. He's on fire now. His skin is melting, blood gushes out of the wounds, and even his clothes are burning. I have no idea what to do.

"Make me cold!" Finn shouts.

"I can't!"

"Yes, you can! Do it!"

There's no time to argue. I think of the coldest spot on Earth, although I've never been there. I work to visualize Finn's body inside a glacier in Antarctica. I can hardly keep the vision going and avoid giving into the panic that wants to take over me. As the seconds tick by, it seems to be working: the flames are gone, his clothes are no longer burning, and his skin is regenerating right before my eyes.

"Drive," he whispers, still clenching his teeth in pain, though not so much as before.

I head down the street, frantically watching the road and Finn. When he touches my arm, something happens. He stops grunting from pain. That perfect day temperature grips my entire body, and I think it soothes him too. I slow down and move to the side of the road, parking right across from the church.

"Come on." I take Finn's arm with one hand

and pull open the glass that separates the front of the truck from the back.

He follows me without debate. In the back, I peel off his burned T-shirt and then his pants. I continue to visualize the Antarctic as we spoon on the bed, my arms wrapped around him. He's almost fully recovered. The parts of his face that were turning to ashes have become flesh again. He had smelled like a rotting corpse, and the sweet scent that normally forms his aroma is back. I know he's recovered when all of a sudden, he's behind me and holding *me*.

He puts his mouth to my ear. "I let my hate get the best of me. That happens sometimes."

"You really hate Exgesis, don't you?" I whisper.

"I do."

"He's pretty wicked."

"Yes, he is."

I turn around to face Finn. I have to see if he's back to normal, and *yes, he is*. "I wonder why this happens when we do this, or even accidentally touch."

"I don't know," he whispers tenderly, which is an un-Finn-like tone.

He kisses my lips in that super sensual way he does. It's truly amazing how he takes his time to relish the moment, making the next moment more intense than the last. As our bodies come together, I can feel that he wants more. He pets the side of my face, cups my chin, and stares into my eyes. I don't know what he's thinking, but he's thinking something.

"What?" I ask, too curious to keep wondering.

"How can I be in love with you?" he whispers.

I can hardly speak. *Is he in love with me?* If he is, that's a good question. We only started speaking three days ago, though he's been in my head since the first time I saw him. Do I love him too? Where's the line between love and lust? Are they intertwined?

We stare into each other's eyes. It doesn't look as though Finn is waiting for me to comment about his declaration of love.

"Can I have you again?" he asks.

Everything I promised myself goes out the window. "Yes," I say breathlessly.

As he lifts my sweater over my head, we both see that I got dressed so fast, I forgot to put on a bra. Finn's eyes are thanking me for it. He puts his mouth on one of my nipples, and the feel of his tongue makes me take in a breath. I gasp again when his fingers play with the other nipple. As I stare at the top of his head and soon into his eyes, I think so many things. Why is he taking his time? I want him inside me already. It's time to merge into his soul.

He's nibbling on my neck when he says, "Why do I want to drink you so badly?"

"My blood?" I whisper, shocked by this revelation.

"Yes." He's still tasting my neck, licking where the largest vein resides. His upper canine teeth are longer and sharper than I've ever seen them, and his erection is hard as a rock. When he breathes, there's a low growl in his throat. He's trembling.

I swallow hard. I don't know what to do. I want him to drink from me if that's possible, but I don't know if it's possible. With another one of those mystery movements that I'm training my eyes to follow, he takes off my pants and panties. Then his underwear is off. I gasp as he thrusts himself inside me. He shifts his hips indulgently. With each movement, my body wants to orgasm. I want to know why that is!

It's not normal.

I hear myself moaning. I clutch his shoulders of steel as I try to contain myself.

"May I drink you?" he asks.

"Yes," I say without hesitation. I'm fully under his spell. If he ends up killing me, it'll be the best death ever.

"Count to ten," he whispers as he pushes deeper inside me and pulls out. "Then tell me to stop."

I swallow hard. "Okay."

He slams his dick back inside me. His sharp teeth pierce my neck. At first it feels like two pinpricks, but the next orgasmic sensation soothes the sting. It's all too much. My eyes shut tight, and I'm losing my mind. My head floats as he sucks blood from my body. I feel as if a potent drug is active in my bloodstream, and it's spreading a pleasurable sensation through my body. He said to count to ten, but I haven't even gotten to one before I scream as I climax.

Finn lets out the loudest growl, and he pulls his teeth out of my neck as he orgasms. I manage to open my eyes so that I can watch him. I can't imagine giving someone that much pleasure, the same amount as he's already brought me. Can we do this forever?

"I told you to tell me to stop," he scolds as he looks down at my face.

"I was getting to it," I lie as I gaze up at his gorgeous face.

"I could've killed you." The skin between his eyes is puckered.

He's admonishing me while screwing me. *Goodness, that's so sexy.* "But you didn't." I smirk at him.

"But I could've."

"But you didn't."

During our silent stare down, he shifts his hips again. Then he lowers his mouth to mine. His tongue and lips have a different taste.

"Wait," I say.

He stops kissing me and draws back as if I've alarmed him.

"The taste in your mouth… Is that me?" I ask.

"Yes. You taste like you smell, and your blood isn't blood."

"Then what is it?"

He lifts his powerful shoulders. "I don't know but—" He stops himself.

"But what?"

"But something is happening to me now."

I frown hard. "What's happening to you?"

"I see you differently."

"Is that good or bad?" I'm worried that I made a mistake by letting my guard down. I love him too —God help me, I do—and I'm worried he's about to turn strange again, as he did yesterday.

"There's something inside you," he says. "It's a key, and it's on fire, and it's on your heart. And…"

"And what?" I ask. I must admit, I'm relieved he's not retreating from me again.

"You have a heart like a human's. Your brain is too…" Then his eyes fall down my body. "But the rest of you is different. You're made different. Like your blood."

We fall silent. I simply don't know how to process his words. If I don't look human on the inside, then what do I look like? Finn frowns as he watches my thoughts through my facial expressions.

Then a voice from the front of the truck says, "You two should get up here."

I know the voice, but Finn glances up toward the front of the truck. "It's the creature who calls himself a Wek."

"Raz, I know," I say, hating his timing.

Finn doesn't appear too happy about being interrupted either; I don't think he was finished with me yet. I'm positive he's a slow and steady lover who gives his all when he makes love. I'm wondering what other woman has shared this experience with Finn. Am I so lucky to be the only one? I doubt it. He's too good to be a virgin. Although he said that he's "old-fashioned" in that he's only with one girl at a time. I smile because right now, I'm that girl.

"Why are you smiling?" Finn asks, beaming.

I'm *so* glad he's happy about what we just did. "I'll tell you later." I'd better slip my clothes on.

He's already up and dressed in a fresh pair of black trousers and T-shirt. "I can help you, if you want."

"Help me do what?"

"Get dressed."

He's smirking. Wow. That's a good look on him. I smirk back, and his eyes gleam like it's a good look on me too.

"Go for it," I dare him. I'm truly curious about how he's going to get this done.

Suddenly I'm moving this way and that, floating in some cases, and before I know it, I'm lying on my back. He's on his side beside me, closing my jeans one button at a time.

"Do you need those?" He glances over his shoulder at my navy blue panties. "I thought we should just keep those off since you're not wearing anything up here." He massages one of my breasts through the sweater he put on me.

We're both caught in the moment. I want him to take my clothes off of me again, and it's evident that he wants to too. Raz knocks impatiently on the window.

"We should go," I whisper.

"Can I love you?" his voice asks inside my head.

"Yes," I whisper without a microsecond of a pause. *Definitely yes.*

Raz is sitting in the middle of the long front seat. After I crawl through the window, I move over to his right, and Finn sits to the left. With Raz between us, the vampire who'd just asked if I'll let him love me seems to be a million miles away. No matter though—it's always good to see Raz.

"Hey," I say and give him a hug. I hold on a little longer than usual as I think about Aries.

Raz lets go of me first. "I'm going to tell you this really fast—you and I are made from the dust of Enu. Aries isn't. But I love her; you know that."

He wasn't asking, but I nod anyway. They are the definition of two people in love, or at least they were. Just thinking about the two in past tense causes a wave of sadness to wash over me.

"It's a long story, but she's in Enu for now."

"Can I can go to this place called Enu?" I ask.

"Anytime, but…" He looks me dead in the eyes. "You can't hang out in Enu now, Glo." He gazes out the front window. "There's a lot going on." Then in Raz-style, he nods, leaving it at that.

Twenty-eight years of knowing Raz has taught me to let him leave it at that. He's not an explainer.

"So, what are we facing?" I point my chin toward the front windshield.

The fog has lifted. Snow is falling. There's not a soul about.

"You saw Lario Exgesis's intentions, didn't you, Glo?" Raz asks.

"His intentions?" I wonder aloud. "Do you mean the sun?"

Raz lifts his mouth into a lopsided smile. "Yes, that's it." He touches my neck at the same spot Finn sunk his teeth into.

I'm a little embarrassed, I must admit. I feel wrong, as if we went too far.

"And he said he doesn't drink humans." Raz turns to glare at Finn, who narrows his eyes at him.

By the way Finn's watching Raz's hand on my neck, what's upsetting him is pretty clear. After Raz stops touching me, Finn blurts, "Why the riddles?"

"This Lario Exgesis, he has ambitions," Raz says in his customary draggy tone. "Obadiah's son, he's all bad. He's not coming back to this town, and he could if he wanted to. You two are done with this here. You have to deal with Exgesis's ambition, and that means getting to Jari before the Selell with the power of the sun leaves it."

"I'm confused," I say.

"Count me as confused too," Finn says.

"Don't you get it, dude? Exgesis wants the sun. He drinks vampires."

I feel my entire face frowning as my brain works. "Wait! A Selell is a vampire, and if he drinks this vampire with the power of the sun, he'll have the power of the sun?"

"So…" Raz scratches the inside corner of his right eyebrow, like he does when something's irritating him. He turns to Finn. "Go ahead. Melt the ice on the window."

Finn frowns at him for a moment, but Raz urges him to go for it. Finn widens his eyes at the windshield, and the ice turns to water until it turns to steam. As new snow falls on to the glass, it sizzles and evaporates.

"If you'd killed Glo, you could've taken her powers from her," Raz says.

"I wasn't going to kill her," Finn barks; he sounds offended.

"I know, dude," Raz says with a nonchalant shrug.

Finn studies him with a deeply perplexed expression. I'm starting to understand what that look means. Finn didn't expect to find me or be attracted to me, let alone make love to me or fall in love with me, and he didn't expect Raz to be so dismissive about him drinking my *precious* blood.

"You said this place is called Jari?" Finn asks. His entire demeanor has changed toward Raz. He's more relaxed.

It's not hard to fall in "like" with Raz. He's a likable guy—or Wek.

"Yeah. This Selell in Jari. He's still contemplating some things, you know? Each minute he wastes is equal to months on Earth."

"What is he contemplating?" I ask. It's just like Raz to leave that part out.

"Becoming human."

"He's a vampire?" Finn's entire body is rigid as he waits for clarification.

"Yeah," Raz says. "And you really need him to stay that way. If he comes back as a human, Lario will have him changed, but he won't be the same kind of Selell."

"He'll be the new breed," Finn says.

"New breed?" Raz muses. "I'll buy that. But if the Selell with the power of the sun is turned into

Lario's kind of vampire and Lario drinks him, Lario will be able to do some devastating stuff."

"Do you know why this is all happening?" Finn asks.

"Kind of." It sounds as though he's going to leave it at that, but then Raz says, "Fawn, one of the sisters, gave him a leaf to eat from the Tree of Life."

"I've heard rumors to that effect," Finn says. "Supposedly he was with a woman who helped him find his way back to humanity. I never believed it though, and I never checked the story out. Exgesis is a pathological liar, and if he's out of my sight, then I keep him out of my mind. But you're saying it was true, and one of Glo's sisters gave him the leaf?"

"Yeah," Raz says.

"But he's a vampire again."

"Yeah."

"And the leaf gave him more power?"

"You got it," Raz replies.

Finn nods, as if it all finally makes sense.

That's when Raz faces me. "I got a map for you." He presses one hand on each side of my forehead. "You have the key. Just follow your instincts."

Then he disappears. Finn and I are left staring

at each other. I don't think I'll ever get used to Raz's ability to vanish. It's as strange as my ability to walk on air or this tugging inside me that's begging me to move forward.

"This is worse than what I thought," Finn says.

I let out a long, mood-resetting sigh. "So do we just leave?"

As I gaze over the town, I see that the people are still inside their homes. There's quite a crowd in the church across the street. A guy at the podium is warning people about the coming of the apocalypse or something. He's saying some scary stuff, and by the looks on the faces of those who are listening to him, it's working.

I grunt. "The apocalypse—is that what we are?"

Finn curls his neck to see what I'm looking at. "To them we are." He starts the truck. "Where to?"

"You should head north toward Dublin, Ohio. At least, that's what I see," I say.

He nods. I smile because he's trusting my instincts.

"What's that smile for?" he asks.

I hesitate. *Should I say it?* "Um… Can I love you too?"

Now he's smiling. "I thought you'd never ask."

I beam as I sigh, relieved.

———

SOON FINN'S ZOOMING NORTH ON THE I-65. THE weather isn't good, but Finn uses his sight to see hundreds of miles in the distance. He decides to take surface streets to avoid the traffic caused by accidents and major road closures up ahead.

I'll admit that I'm extremely antsy. The closer we get to sundown, the more my stomach turns, and it's not even noon yet. My head is filled with all the stuff Raz told us. We have to retrieve a vampire with the power of the sun from this place called Jari, and I somehow have the key to this place inside me. But it doesn't stop there. After drinking my blood, Finn had said he saw light in the shape of a key against my heart. How creepy is that? Who in the world has something like that lingering inside them?

"Hey," Finn says, interrupting my train of thought.

I turn to face him, and after a moment, he pulls me toward him.

"What's going on with you?" he asks.

I remember him telling me not to let him know

that I'm afraid. I understand that if he's worried about me, then it's harder for him to concentrate on the mission at hand. "I'm just thinking about those people in Lo Creek. We just left, you know?" I hate lying.

"Don't worry about them. They'll figure it out. They always do."

"And what about Obadiah's son?"

Finn gives that some thought. "I'll keep an eye out for him."

I flinch, taken aback. "How do you know what he looks like?"

"I figured Obadiah had photos of his son around the house, so I got his address from his wallet."

"You did all of that just by using your eyes?"

"Don't worry, Glo. Pretty soon, it'll be instinctive for you too."

I press my cheek against his chest. "You certainly think of things that I would never—"

That's all I'm able to say before our truck comes to an abrupt stop along the side of the road. After a series of moves, he's lying on top of me on the front seat of the truck.

"Here's where you have the advantage," he whispers.

I stare at his conflicted expression, but I can feel what he means between his legs.

"I can't control this desire I have for you." His voice trembles. "You'll have to be careful with me for a while. Okay?"

I gulp. "Okay."

He doesn't move an inch, as if he's taking extra care to be still. After a minute of him lying on top of me, staring into my eyes with our lips practically touching, he moves back behind the steering wheel and steps on the gas. I stay on my side of the truck even though he's the one who initially moved me closer to him. I'm not confused, but I can't help but wonder...

"When was the last time you... um..." I turn toward him. "Were with someone? Sexually?"

"About an hour ago," he says with a coy grin.

I chuckle. I'm sort of surprised Finn made a joke. One of the things I've learned about him is he's not the humorous type. However, I do know he's the literal type. He answers questions in the context that they're asked. So I rephrase.

"Okay." I roll my eyes a little. "When was the last time you had sex with someone other than me?"

His eyes narrow again, and his mouth tightens. He's thinking. "Four and a half years ago."

"Really?" I'm taken aback. From the way he behaves when we have sex, I figured it was more like a hundred or two hundred, maybe three hundred years ago. "Vampire or human?"

"Vampire."

I notice him frown harder. He's thinking again, possibly remembering her. He said he's old-fashioned, only loving one woman at a time.

"Did you fall out of love with her?" I feel as if I'm pressuring him, but I'm eager to know it all.

After a long moment of silence filled by only the hum of the engine, he says, "No."

"Then you still love her?" I practically shout. My heart is on the verge of accusing him of misleading me. But I know Finn would never do that. There's something deeper to the story; I just have to continue digging.

"No," he whispers. He turns to study my face. "She's dead."

"Oh." I gulp. "Sorry."

He takes my hand again. "Don't be. I love her, but not like I love you. This is all new for me. What we have is inexplicable."

I nod and close my eyes to sigh. "I know. What was her name?"

Again, he hesitates. "Gia."

"Pretty name," I say. "Where did you meet her?"

He shifts uncomfortably. I know I'm pushing him. If he chooses not to answer, then I'll understand.

"She was a Siren," he says, looking more conflicted than he did a second ago.

I want to let it drop, but now I'm even more curious. "You mean, like, a 'hot' girl?" I use my fingers to show the quotes.

"No, like a Siren."

I frown harder, trying to figure out what in the world he was referring too. Was she an inanimate object?

He glances at me. "You ever read Greek mythology?"

Suddenly, it clicks. "You mean a Seirên? One of three goddesses who lured ships to their destruction?" I frown hard, remembering. "Didn't they drown or something?"

"That's a myth."

"Well, I know," I say. "But you told me she's a Siren like in Greek mythology, so…"

"Some myths and legends are born from reality."

I take a deep, calming breath. I don't want to argue about how he's confusing me. I work to remain composed. "So were you once a sailor?"

"No," he says with a smirk. "I was a vampire. I met her in a tavern in Greece, and she seduced me."

"Oh," I say, watching him with a wide-eyed expression.

She seduced him. I wonder how that occurred. I can see a sultry mythical creature in a seedy bar making all the right moves on Finn. I've never made any moves on him, and I think I'm feeling a pinch of jealousy. I would've loved to seduce him. How fun that would have been.

He glances at me with the most sincere expression. "If I ever had to choose between you or Gia, it would be you."

"Why me?" I can't help but ask. "Because from what I read, a Siren has serious power over men."

"Because…" I can see him thinking again. "When I touch you, forever doesn't seem like hell on Earth anymore."

"How do you know I'm going to live forever?"

He graces me with a lazy but sexy smile. "Experience."

I chuckle at joke number two. What can I say to that, other than I want him to take me to the back of his truck and screw my brains out? I stare at the side of his face. He's fighting to avoid eye contact. I wonder if he feels my desire for him?

"We're going to have to keep our heads in the game," he says.

That's when I take my eyes off of him. "I know."

Finn doesn't say anything, nor does he look my way for the next few hours. Whenever I get a quick glimpse of him, he's staring straight ahead. It's fine though, because although the thought of food still makes me nauseated, I'm a little tired.

"I guess I'll go lie down," I say and start to crawl over the back seat.

Finn grabs my thigh and shakes his head. "No. Please stay up here."

I'm on the verge of protesting until I remember how strange Finn is. I see the lust burning in his eyes when he looks at me, and there's no time better than the present to learn how to control our cravings for each other.

"Okay," I whisper.

He quickly takes his hand off my thigh. I strap myself into my seat and snuggle against the door before closing my eyes. Normally I can tell myself to sleep and off I go, but right now, I'm too aware of Finn. Truth be told, I don't want to slumber. I want to stay aware of his presence for as long as I can.

My ears tune into the purr of the engine and the sound of snow beating on the hood. From there, I wonder about this vampire who's debating about whether or not to become human. I didn't know a vampire could be changed back. I thought they had to die. And what happens to them when they become, as they say, a creature of the night? Don't they turn all gooey and congealed inside?

I could see right through Finn if I wanted to. How come I've never let my eyes go there? I'm playing with the possibility of looking. I turn around to face him only to see that he's staring at me while maintaining complete control of the vehicle. Suddenly, I forget why I turned around in the first place. His eyes and even his mouth are hypnotizing.

I thumb over my shoulder. "Listen, Finn, I really think I need to lie down."

"But it's cold back there," he says.

"There are blankets."

He pulls me near him. "Just wait. We're almost there."

I frown, confused. "Almost where?"

"A place to stop until sundown."

"We're stopping?"

"We're wasting time driving. Once we're out of the daylight, we can travel faster."

He's right, of course. I know we can't drive to where we have to go. I've been given a direct route, and there's no highway or road involved. We need to travel across the woods and small towns, cities, and rolling hills. Something tells me that when we get to the entrance of Jari, we'll have to be ready for a fight.

CHAPTER 10
EXIT JARI

"Portland, Tennessee," I whisper, thinking aloud while noticing the name of the small town we're driving through. It's very, very green here, and we're rolling down a quiet street with quaint, ranch-style homes set far from the road.

"Not a fan?" Finn asks me.

I shrug. "I don't know. I'm not into the South, regardless how it shakes down. City"—I look at a field of green grass sprinkled with trees under a gray and threatening sky—"or this."

He smirks as he turns the truck down an easy-to-miss dirt road. Tall, bushy trees stacked three deep line both sides of the narrow road. I'm really curious about where he's taking us. In no time at all, I see a white shack at the end of the muddy path. Once we get close enough, the garage door lifts. Finn drives inside, and it closes behind us. It's pitch black in here, but I'm getting used to seeing with my second sight. Now that we're stopped, he reaches under the seat and hands me a plastic box with little white pills in it.

"The Zombies," I say, shocked he grabbed them before fleeing the Shack.

Finn winks and opens his door. Within a second, we're both out of the truck, and his body is pressed against mine—and so are his lips. He's been so careful kissing me until now. This kiss is greedy, and I match his intensity. My head spins as it usually does when we make contact.

He takes the box before I drop it and lifts me so that I can wrap my legs around his waist. I can't get close enough to him. When I see his fangs protruding, I pull my hair back and twist my neck for him to drink. *Please, drink.*

Finn just stares at the swollen vein until he lowers his mouth to kiss it. "You give it away so easily. Glo, I could kill you. You have to believe that."

"But you won't." I kiss around his mouth, which is struggling against kissing me back at the moment.

"Not if we do it right, but if we lose control… If *I* lose control…"

I stop pelting him with kisses to ask, "You're really into that, aren't you?"

"Into what?"

"Self-control."

"It's discipline," he says as my feet hit the ground. "We have to function with some of it." He shakes the box of Zombies. "Starting with these."

That's Finn changing the subject, but I'm not ready to do that.

"*You* kissed *me*," I say. "You're always kissing me first, touching me first, and then *you* either lose control or push me away."

"Yes," he confesses. "How can I say this?" He wraps an arm around my back and stares into my eyes.

Once again, I can't breathe or swallow, and I'm certain I'm about to pass out. I'm immobilized by the force of his eyes, but this time, I try to steady my breathing and get a grip.

"I want you all the time, every single second. I want to go in there"—he points at the back of the truck with his chin—"and make love to you for a very long time. Hell, I want to forget about the vampire with the power of the sun and wherever that leads us and just stay in bed and be inside you. Kissing you is not enough. Touching you isn't either. If I drink your blood now, I won't stop. I have to be inside you to be sure I'll stop." He studies my expression. I'm not sure what my face is showing him, but he asks, "Do you understand?"

I swallow before I croak, "I do."

He slides a finger across my bottom lip and then takes two steps back from me. "Good, because we have somewhere to be before the sun goes down."

I follow Finn behind the truck. Between the bumper and the white plaster wall is a hatch in the ground. Finn lifts it.

"Are you ready?" he asks.

I gaze into the hole. There's nothing but black down there, and using my first sight, I can't see a bottom. That makes me squeamish about jumping into the hole, but I nod. "Yes."

To my surprise, I don't have to jump. Finn wraps his arms around me, and I hold on tight as we fall into the gorge together. When I look up, I see that the hatch has closed. It seems as if we've been dropping for a long time, but we have not. The darkness is so eerie. I'm so petrified that I'd rather not use my eyes to *really* see what's around us.

Water splashes when Finn's feet hit the ground. We're in a wet, chilly tunnel. The soles of my boots sink into the shallow but stale water. I mean, one sniff is enough to knock a person out.

"What's down here?" I ask with my nose turned up.

"Get on my back," Finn instructs me.

I waste no time following orders. *"Is this how vampires travel during the day?"* I choose not to speak out loud for fear of being overheard by the sewer monster that probably only exists in my head.

"Yes," he says, and then we're off.

I keep my eyes open as we journey at Finn's speed. I've already trained my eyes to keep up with him, so although it's pitch-black, I can see that the walls are made of cement and are caked with rust and dust. I might hurl at any second. It's the smell; I can barely take it.

Finn moves so fast that I know we're definitely not in Tennessee anymore. My instincts are turning inside me, letting me know that we're very close to our destination. All of a sudden, Finn slows until he's walking at regular speed. This part of the tunnel doesn't smell as bad. My arms are still wrapped tightly around Finn's neck, and he's carrying me as if I weigh zero pounds. I might as well be a flea on his back. He stops at a dead end and turns to the wall to our left.

Once I get a good look of what's beyond the wall, I understand what he's going to do next. The cement turns to dust, and we walk into a tiny, well-lit room. Finn puts the wall back together in the same amount of time it took to pulverize it.

"I can put you down here," Finn says, looking at the cleaner cement floor.

I don't want to slide off of his back, but I do. It's time to stand on my own two feet, literally and figuratively.

"What's here?" I ask while searching beyond the boundaries. Nothing but soil surrounds us. I tilt my head to gaze up, and I see how the height of this room runs very deep.

A thunderous howl echoes in the space. My heart races, and I plant my feet firmly as I brace for another fight. I gaze upward, waiting for the attack, but there's nothing or no one coming.

"Follow me," Finn calmly says. He lifts himself off the ground and travels upward.

He's not moving as fast as he normally does; he's going at a pace I can keep up with. So I let myself believe I can walk on air, and I do it. We move up, up, up. Before we reach the top of the room, Finn stops at a metal door that's painted white. It opens without him touching it.

"Stay close," Finn whispers before we walk into what looks like an abandoned parking garage.

We walk to the middle of the area and stand out in the open. Finn steps in front of me at the same time a guy appears out of nowhere.

"Elo," the guy says to Finn.

That must be his last name. Finn Elo.

"Chex," Finn says in return.

I'm pretty sure this is their greeting. Chex curves his neck to get a good look at me behind Finn. His eyes go from curious to ablaze in less than two seconds.

"Keep your eyes on me," Finn barks at him.

Although Chex tries to look away from me, he can't. It's strange. I feel as if I could be his dinner, but now that I've gotten used to using my powers, I'm confident I could easily take him down. He has sharp black eyes, white skin, and black hair. His lips are very pink though, sort of puerile. I don't have to question whether or not he's a vampire. There's a hunger in his eyes that gives away his desires. He wants to sink his teeth into my neck and suck every ounce of my blood. *That* I'm sure of.

Finn shoves the plastic box of Zombies at him. "Here."

I can hardly see Chex's hand move as he takes the box, opens it, and sniffs one of the pills.

"All I can smell is her," he says, narrowing his eyes at me.

The next thing I know, Finn's hand is around Chex's neck and squeezing. "Well, try again." He growls through his clenched teeth and then lets Chex go.

Chex must be able to smell what Finn finds so delicious about me. He's unable to concentrate on whatever business he and Finn are transacting because he can't keep his eyes off me. That means I have to stay on guard, so like a hawk, I watch his every move.

"Is that the same drug that was given to the humans in Scatheshire?" Finn asks.

This time, the vampire closes his eyes and sniffs it. "That's it."

"There's a connection then."

"Seems so," the vampire answers, studying me.

"Hey." Finn snaps his finger to regain Chex's attention. It works. "The Scatheshires were used to attack the Catskill Coven, right?"

The vampire blinks hard, and he's shaking a little. I get the feeling that at any moment, he's going to lose whatever control he has.

"Chex, right?" Finn grabs both of his shoulders.

I think it's an attempt to steady him. Then it happens.

I see Finn flying through the air, and then Chex moves toward me. He has me by the shoulders and his mouth is open, but I hit him with fire—lava kills faster than fire. He falls to the cement, rolling and crying out in agony as his body smokes from head to toe. I stand over him, just to let him know who's doing this to him. When I feel he's caught my drift, I take the fire off of him and visualize him covered in ice. However, for my safety, I keep the lava walls around me.

When Chex recovers, he stands and wiggles to sort of shake off what just happened to him. I turn to look at Finn, and he has the biggest smile. I've never seen him smile that big. Then, in an instant, he's standing beside me, still grinning from ear to ear.

"I forgot to warn you about trying that, but I guess experience is the best lesson," Finn says.

"Fuck you, Elo. She could've killed me," Chex roars.

"You tried to drink her," Finn says in my defense.

"Fuck it," Chex hisses and only focuses on Finn. Thanks to the heat, he acts as though I'm not in the vicinity. "I got word that they're calling whatever they're planning 'The Assault.'"

"An assault on who?" Finn asks.

"Hell if I know. But all the old vampires are steering clear of the newbies. They've got no damn boundaries." His eyes flicker to me when he says that, probably because he'd just crossed a boundary. He lifts a hand and mutters, "Sorry. Couldn't help it."

I grimace at him. I'm quite confused by his apology. I'm quick to let bygones be bygones, but I'm not sure if I should let my guard down with him. "Apology accepted."

Finn digs in his pants pocket and slips out what looks to be a credit card. "Here you go." He hands the card to Chex. "Keep me posted as best you can on the Assault."

Chex nods at him, then at me, and then he's gone.

Finn studies me for a moment. "You're starting to learn, but next time, don't let them get that close."

"You knew he was going to attack me?"

Finn stares into my eyes. "A vampire will always attack you. Especially Chex. He's a sniffer."

"A sniffer?"

"He knows what everything and every person in this world smells like. He can track origins, put scents together, and tell me who's involved with whom."

"Wow," I say. "And he works for you?"

"No, he works *with* me. When Chex was turned into a vampire, he was a royal assassin."

"Really? For whom?" I'm so eager to know the answer that I'm like a puppy waiting for a bacon bit.

"Can't tell you. I promised him."

"But you know who?" I ask, still sounding overzealous.

"I do."

It's apparent that's all he's willing to say about it, so I nod. "Very interesting." I'll respect his wishes and leave it at that.

"We should go. You should lead us," Finn says when he rips his eyes away from my face.

I gulp. "I should?"

He avoids looking at me when he says, "You can do it. Just look around and take us to where we need to go."

After a deep sigh, I tell myself I can do it, especially if Finn is convinced that I can. He's putting a lot of trust in me, and I kind of love it. I slowly shuffle in circles, observing the routes that shoot out around us. There are so many passageways, but I feel a tug within me leading me toward one exit. I choose to trust it.

"This way," I whisper and shoot off in the direction my instincts carry me.

This time, it's Finn who follows. Our association is beginning to feel like a partnership.

WE'RE MOVING FAST DOWN LONG TUNNELS THAT look and smell like sewers. Sometimes we journey deeper into the earth and sometimes higher. Every now and then, we have to stop to avoid running into other vampires who are skulking through the dank pathways.

"What are they looking for?" I ask Finn as we're held up in a dark crevice.

"Luck," he answers.

Then he does something I don't expect. He puts his lips to mine and gives me a tender kiss.

"Sorry, couldn't help it," he says.

Once my head settles, I take a deep breath. Even though I'm not using my mouth, I can hardly say, *"We're going straight up this path, and then we're there."*

Finn turns to use his super peripheral vision to see the path I just laid out. *"It's fifty-three miles north."* Then he looks up. *"Sundown is three hours away."*

I see that burning look in his eyes, but before I finish blinking, Finn has grabbed me. We're off at his speed. He's taking us off the path a bit, destroying and rebuilding boundaries as we move. We even cut through dark soil. It all happens so fast, but we end up in a chamber of four solid steel walls. There's a full-sized bed and one floor-to-ceiling wooden cabinet in here. Unlike the rest of the underworld we've just traveled through, the entire room already holds the scent of Finn Elo.

"Do you sleep here?" I ask. I notice he hasn't let me go yet.

"Sometimes," he barely says while staring into my eyes.

Then he slips off my coat. Although it's freezing in this room, I'm warm from head to toe because he keeps one arm curled around my lower back. He slips my sweater over my head with the other hand and then unbuttons my jeans.

What's lovely about the reality of Finn and me is even in this pitch-black room, we can see each other as clear as day. Who would have thought I'd ever meet someone with the same ability as me? Someone who takes my breath away every time he touches me.

"Can I make love to you, Glo?" he whispers near my mouth and waits for my answer.

"Yes."

My back smashes into the mattress. Finn has already undressed the both of us, and his rock-hard penis has entered me. His thrusts are so indulgent. I wonder if he knows that there's a constant low whimper in his throat. Or if he knows how very gently his body shivers during the act. But I'm unable to remain so aware of all that Finn does because I can no longer keep my head. The pleasure is so extraordinary that it's hardly tolerable. I could do this forever—while taking breaks between orgasms of course. Right here in this room with no food, no light, no other soul—just the two of us. When I feel the orgasm building and building and peaking, I can't help but whimper loudly.

Never have I made so much noise during sex! But I can't help it, and I can hardly stand the pleasure. When I'm able to open my eyes even a tiny bit, I see that Finn is studying every contour of my face. He puts his mouth on mine as I let out the final and loudest cry. In my past dealings with men, they would take this opportunity to let go and end it, but not Finn. After I climax, he continues.

My body responds to him, which is also odd. Normally after experiencing such a fantastic orgasm, I'd need to recover and take the time to build up to the next. But what's going on between us is like a transformation of my anatomy. It's like a gift of our bonding, and a curse too. Because we can't do this forever. At the moment, we only have until the sun drops. After that, we have a job to do.

As the hours pass, Finn's tongue tastes every inch of my body. My nipples are decidedly his favorite. He can't get enough of them, nor can he get enough of tasting my nectar. He's so intense and sensual about experiencing me that I give him full control. His tongue circles my clit, round and round—it's a sensual assault. I scream as the explosion squeezes me, and he doesn't let up. His tongue probes me, sliding in and out, in and out, in and... I scratch at the sheets, grab his shoulders, and pant relentlessly.

He lifts my lower half and stabs me with the full length of his firmness. "Shit," he whimpers as he thrusts. "Shit."

When he lets out the final growl and I the final whimper, he positions me on top of him while remaining inside me. We gaze into each other's eyes. I know what he's thinking, and I'm sure he knows what I'm thinking. This is it. From this moment on, we're together for life.

"WE HAVE TWENTY MINUTES," FINN WHISPERS AS I see my opportunity to take charge.

I shift my hips back and forth, and he's responding.

"You should drink some of my blood," I whisper, feeling the tickling of another orgasm soon to explode inside me.

Finn turns his head to look off in the horizon. "Look at where we're going."

I let my eyes follow his line of sight. Vampires lurk around the exit my instincts lead us to. They're waiting for sundown too. I guess someone's pretty sure the vampire with the power of the sun will show up there.

"Are they new breed?" I ask Finn.

"They are. But don't worry about them. Never worry about the future. Stay in the present."

He lifts his mouth to mine, and we're rolling around the bed kissing. My time in control is short-lived, because he's back on top of me. His teeth sink into my neck. As the liquid that's not quite blood, according to Finn, leaves me and enters him, I'm once again floating.

One, two, three, four, five, six, seven, eight, nine, ten...

"Stop," I force myself to whisper.

Right away, Finn's teeth are out of my neck, and he's smirking. "Very good, Glo." He sounds like a teacher speaking to a good student. "Now let's get you dressed."

With only a few minutes to spare, I'm laughing out of my head. Finn dresses me again like he did in the truck. I love that he's smiling more. He lets down his guard with me, and I love that. It's safe for him to be this way with me because I'll never hurt him. Once again, he takes his time buttoning my jeans as I lay back on the bed.

"Forty-five seconds," he whispers before kissing one of my nipples through the sweater. "Forty." He kisses the other one.

I find myself on my feet and giggling as he gives my nipples one more grope. He reluctantly puts my coat on me and zips it.

"Twenty seconds," he says. He's the only naked one in the room.

My goodness, what an illustrious body he has. However, he's not naked for long.

"Fifteen seconds," he says, now fully clothed. "Hop on."

I climb on his back, and without a pause, we take off. I find a lot of value in the walls of lava I erected around myself yesterday, so I put them around us now. The scent of mint and lime disappears.

The other vampires who have found the caves move fast, but Finn is quicker. We slash right past them on our way up an abandoned well. We climb out of the belly of the earth until we're heading toward the night sky. Vampires surround us, and they've already sniffed out the difference between us and them. However, Echo Leon's found his way here too. His blade is working, making sure we have a clear path toward the slit of light that's so blinding, even using my second sight, I have to squint at it.

"Do you see it?" I ask Finn, almost yelling in his head.

"I do!" Finn bolts ahead.

The vampires that slam into the lava walls fall off, howling in agony. At one point, I see Finn watching it happen, and he's smirking. The closer we get to the tear in the sky, the faster we go. On impact, Finn and I are pulled apart. My entire body glows until light pushes out of my pores, my mouth, and my eyes. Panic grips me. *What's happening?* I kick and wiggle, trying to regain control of my limbs.

But then the blinding light becomes my soother. It pets me and hugs me, whispering, "You're safe."

Once I stop struggling, I look down and see the greenest woods and grass beneath me. I'm relieved because I also see Finn beside me. We're watching each other, still sort of dazed by this phenomenal experience.

"Is this Jari?" he asks before our feet touch the ground.

"I think so," I answer as we land. "But we're not where we need to be."

I give into my need to run and run fast. I feel Finn behind me, respecting the pace I've set because even my swiftest hardly matches his. The pure, clean air and the velvet blue sky refuse to go unnoticed. There's a peace here that doesn't exist in the world we just left. I've never seen such green trees or grass. Well, maybe in a snow globe. This forest is endless. I'm waiting for a change of scenery the farther we progress, but there isn't one.

Then I see one. Up ahead is a tree with crystal leaves, and silver liquid bubbles all around it. The sight makes me stop in my tracks and blink hard. This cannot be real. I'm almost convinced that it's a dream when I open my eyes to see a vampire, who's not Finn, standing in front of me.

"You're one of the sisters," he says before I can speak.

After a moment, I say, "That's what I've heard. How did you know?"

The vampire is still studying me. "You all look exactly alike." Then he motions with his hands. "Other than your skin, hair, and eyes. It's the most intense thing I've ever seen."

I'm not sure I heard him correctly. "You're saying we actually look alike?"

"Like twins." He looks at me curiously. "Is that

why they sent you here? Thinking a new, hot sister can talk me out of it?"

"Talk you out of what?"

"Well, I'm not doing it, so…"

Finn steps up to the edge of the bubbling liquid and stares into it. He waves me over. "Glo, look at this."

I go stand beside him to see what's got him so fascinated, and I gasp.

Three worlds are down there. The first appears to have been destroyed by fire or something. The ground is covered with ashes, and charred skeletal trees are scattered throughout the terrain. Shadows in the form of humans fly across the moonless, starless, bleak sky. To the east of that world lies another world that's gloomier than the first. It's sort of developed. I see brick huts and fires burning in fissures within a very dense, dark forest. The woods surround a massive ancient ruin made of clay. It's so tall that the top of it seems to scratch a sky that's blacker than the center world. To the west of the first world, a thick wall of light separates the center world from a place where the mountains are made of crystal and the streams are clear as glass. The beauty of this third world is unbelievable. It has trees with crazy colored leaves, like pink, purple, blue, and even silver.

"What in the world?" Finn marvels, gaping at everything I see.

"What's going on?" the other vampire asks, now standing next to Finn.

Finn and I look at each other with wide eyes.

"There's a lot going on beneath us," I say.

The vampire with the power of the sun's face drops. His eyes grow dim as he stares into the liquid. "It's still there?" His voice shakes a little.

"What's there?" I ask.

"Hell."

Finn and I look at each other, perplexed. Without being asked, I focus on the ground all around us and let myself see through the green grass. Hundreds of feet beneath us lies nothing but pure darkness. At least, that's all I see. Finn's eyes widen in shock.

"What?" I ask.

He narrows his eyes at me. "You don't see that?"

I take a deeper look and then a wider one. "I don't see anything but blackness."

There goes that confused face of his again. I haven't seen that expression in a while.

"What do you see?" I ask.

He locks eyes with the vampire with the power of the sun. Whatever Finn sees, he's seen it too.

"Is it hell?" I ask, studying both of them.

Finn narrows his eyes at me. "No."

"All right." I see that I touched a nerve, so I look at the other vampire. "If you bathe in that liquid, it'll turn you human, right?"

"Yeah," he whispers, still staring at Finn.

There's something in the darkness below that I can't see, but Finn could. Whatever it is has this vampire spooked. I decide to remain silent and let them have their moment.

Something squawks in the sky. We all look up. At first, I see a red bird, then a flock of fowl with blue heads and yellow bodies. Hundreds of them circle around us for a few laps and fly off. The longer we stand here, the more alive this world becomes.

"Are you sure you don't want to do it?" Finn asks the other vampire.

"I don't think it matters if I do or I don't," he says.

"From what I gather, if you're human, you'll still have the power of the sun. There's a vampire who's looking for you right now. Did you know that?" I ask.

The vampire frowns really hard. He appears to be trying to guess who's looking for him. "Do you mean Baron?"

There's a flicker of recognition in Finn's eyes. "Ze Feldis?"

"Yeah, that's his name. Baron Ze Feldis."

"You know him?" Finn asks.

"He's with Clarity." The vampire looks at me. "Your sister. They left here about five minutes ago. In this place's time at least. Your father was here too, and he said that we'd already lost about four Earth years, so I've probably lost a couple of months more."

Now my heart is beating harder. "I've heard that name before. Aries mentioned her."

"Ah, you're the last sister." He shakes his head. "I imagine now all hell's about to break loose."

"Because of me?" I feel my entire face frowning hard. Heck, hell has already broken loose. Does he mean there's more to come? I find this terribly disturbing.

"Because of all of us," he says.

He goes on to tell us his name is Vayle, and he's from Illinois. He used to attend the University of Maine before he became a vampire, and he tells us about how he found my sister named Zill. He says they traveled through the air and slept in an arctic field before fighting shadow spirits in a desert. He leads us through their battles, even the one at a gate that led them to this world, which used to be dark and burnt up. Once he gets to the part in which he and Ze Feldis were pulled into the ground, that disturbed expression appears on his face again. He doesn't talk about what happened there, but he does mention that souls were probably down there. That's where he leaves it, and so does Finn.

"Vayle," Finn says, "we have to get you out of here safe and alive. If you're going to jump into that liquid, do it now so we can go."

"I said I'm not doing it," Vayle snaps.

"Good." Finn stares off into the distance.

I can't help but study him adoringly. He's so dominant, but at the same time, he knows when to step back and let the head that's wisest lead. If all men were so lucky. Heck, if all women were as lucky as me to be bonded to someone like him. I'm still observing him when his entire face frowns.

"Damn, it's daylight again," he says.

"You can see that?" Vayle asks. He sounds shocked.

"Yes." I turn to see how the sun has risen to

high noon beyond this universe. "We'll just have to wait it out."

Vayle shakes his head. "No way. I have the power of the sun."

Finn and I look at him, even more confused.

"I can go out in the daylight. Baron could go out in the day too, as long as I was in the earth." Vayle wiggles a finger between the two of us. "Since you two are together like Baron and Clarity, maybe it works the same for you. At least until we get to the house."

"There's a house?" I ask.

"Yeah." Vayle points toward a certain lit slit in the sky. "It's that way."

Finn and I turn to see outside of this universe and into a forest. There, the sun dips a little to the west, marking the late afternoon of what looks like a very warm day.

"Is that Earth?" I ask, puzzled by the difference between the forest and the rest of Earth.

"It is, but the seasons are different there. Clarity explained it, but I still don't get it."

"Is she there?" I feel my heart tighten again. I'm overeager to see this Clarity.

"Yeah, I think so," he says, nodding. "She and

Ze Feldis are kind of serious, so they're always trying to figure stuff out."

"Is Ze Feldis there?" Finn asks.

"Wherever she goes, he goes." Vayle snorts sarcastically. "I guess I'm the only vampire whose *bond* is in love with a Wek," he mumbles.

"Then take us to Ze Feldis," Finn insists, ignoring Vayle's last comment. Finn's face is all business. He's on a mission now, which is to figure out what the Assault is, and he's not the kind of man who slows down to smell the roses. Whatever his plan is, he needs Vayle in order to carry it out.

"One more thing," I say, because it hardly makes sense to send Finn and me to collect this vampire if he were on his way back to the house, which looks more like an estate. "Where were you going before we showed up?"

"Home," he says. "Just for a little while. I wanted to see my mom one more time. But then I was going to go back to the house and join everybody, I swear."

"Which way is home?" I ask.

Vayle points toward where we entered this land of Jari. Now it all makes sense. Exgesis's vampires would've definitely taken him if we hadn't diverted him from his plan. *Score one for Raz.*

So we follow Vayle, and one by one, we enter the daylight. At first, Finn glares up at the sun, which lords over a cold, snowy day. But when we step into the forest, into the warmth, he looks up again. This time, Finn's face holds the softest expression. But it's just like Finn not to maintain it for long. He stares straight ahead. He knows whom he wants to see and where he needs to go, and we *are* on our way there. All three of us.

———

Keep on the journey! Read the next book in the series .

Read Ignite, Book 5 Now!